SOLITAIRE

by
Albert Samuel Tukker

You can find more information about, and works by Albert S. Tukker at
http://AlbertSamuelTukker.com

ISBN 978-0-557-02468-1

Copyright ASTukker 2005

Welcome,
to my world.
- AST

Table of Contents

Page	Title
5	*Fences*
8	*Alone*
12	*SmokeStone*
107	*Pillow Fight*
112	*Pipe Dream*

Fences

 Throughout it all, it's been only me. There's been no spectres in the darkness, no bumps in the night. Just emptiness. Like a field...
  ...barren of everything, except heat and dust...
Halfway to the horizon there's movement. A bandanna is wiped across the face, folded, then tied around the head.
Imperceptible legs step forward. A drag on a cigarette that wasn't there a moment ago, gone again.
 Exhale.
 There's men. Five of them, all of them in bib overalls. Large men in bulk, but squatty in height, hunched. No shirts, the exposed skin blistering grotesquely. They're tearing down a heavy wooden fence.
 Approaching the fence. Trunk-sized posts, aged and scarred by storms, stretches into the distance to the right. On the left, a thin, jagged line - littered sparsely with mishandled

posts.

Spotted.

The men stop working.

Another drag, gone.

They have fear in their eyes. One glances behind the remaining fence, then disappears in the same direction.

Reaching the scene.

They drop their tools and back away.

Peeking around the fence, the heart quickens.

A car, without wheels, hovers, facing the fence. One gull-wing door opened on the near side, the worker and a dark spectacled woman in conversation beneath it. She looks this way, then exits the craft.

"Come no further."

She speaks, too. Nice.

"Let me see your papers."

'Papers?' I say.

Her head drops. She's frustrated.

'Hold on.' Really nice. Wonder what color eyes? She's dressed in the same type overalls as the fence men. She too, is shirtless. Her breasts fill the garment with reserved sensuality. Her skin is dark brown, without blisters. Patting my bare chest for papers, curiosity induces a visual inventory.

Looking down:

Half-naked. Ammunition belt, shouldered rifle; inverted. No shirt, deep tan. A waist belt with knife, pistol, canteen and small satchel filled with food. Faded bellbottom blue jeans lead to bare feet. In the left back pocket, the papers required.

'What's going on?' I ask.

"This fence is no longer needed. It's being removed."

'Oh.' Minutes pass. 'Why was it put up in the first place?'

She flips a page over, studies it. Delicate fingers.

"Well, you have clearance if you can show need."

She peers out over her glasses, eyes questioning. They are light blue, a clear blue that gave her eyes a breathless depth. Yet, they were haunting in their mist.

'I live on this side.'

She removes her glasses. Peering into her eyes I'm falling...

    falling... through the mirrors of her soul
        lost...in the depths of mine
            ...spectre's in the darkness

Drag.

    Exhale.

        Gone.

Alone

Alone. Yes. Alone. I've been alone since birth. I've been alone in this room all my life, these two windows my only contact with the outside world. But, can I believe what passes these portals? Can I believe what comes in through the acoustical walls?

My room, let me try to describe it to you. It won't take long, it's not very large. It is oblong, tall and bare. Only a single chair that sits centered between the windows occupies any floor space. The floor is wood, scratched and marred. The walls are opaque, not quite solid, yet impenetrable. Only sounds passes through them. Their colours change with the scene outside the window, or for no reason at all, like a neurotic chameleon. I've yet to discover a door, but at night, I dream of being on the other side, roaming through an immense labyrinth. But, as I sit in the darkness of pre-dawn, I can't shake

Alone

the feeling of a vast emptiness just on the other side of the walls.

The dreams, though, that's what I'm here to tell you about. The dreams. Last nights' was the same. Though they're not the same. Last night...

I was walking down a narrow corridor with high walls and no ceiling, the half-light filtering in from above, stars peppering the black void. In the distance, the direction unknown, I heard a sound. It wasn't much of a sound, like a muffled murmur. I walked a little faster, peering down every corner I came across. A scent drifted to me, a familiar smell I never smelled before. I walked faster still, nearing a run. I called out, "Who's there...?"

No answer. I ran, calling again. No answer. I began to sweat, partly from exercise, partly from fear. Who had invaded my realm? The sound came again, louder this time. I stopped and listened. I could discern a direction. I ran to the next corner, turned and stopped.

There before me, dressed in blue jeans and a white silk blouse was a woman, her skin light caramel, smooth and young. She was tall and slim, her jeans tattered; frayed at the bottom with a hole in one knee. Her blouse was loose, unbuttoned to her waist where it was tucked cross-tailed into the jeans. Her breasts were small so the loose blouse revealed nothing but flat chest. The long sleeves billowed to the buttons fastened at her wrists. She was barefoot and her black mane hung loosely below her shoulders.

I took a few steps closer, until her face could be seen. She was beautiful. A small, wide nose and thin lips highlighted her warm, brown eyes. They laughed and whispered as she

Alone

pulled me into them. She smiled slowly, raising her arms to me, beckoning me to her.

I asked her name, wanting to hear her voice.

"Come to me, Sebastion, before it's too late," she said softly. Her voice soothing, pleasant.

I went to her, taking her hands in mine, the warmth unfamiliar in my one room world. I wrapped my arms around her, and she enveloped me in hers. I melted into her. I felt our hearts touch and begin to beat in unison. I looked into her eyes and saw her soul, and suddenly, I knew everything about her. She moved her hands up my back, pulling me closer. Our lips touched. Our minds entwined, our souls merged. My hands found their way inside her blouse. Her skin was soft, warm, alive. I could feel the blood pulsing beneath it. She removed my shirt. I laid her gently on the floor. Again, I asked her her name...

I awoke to find myself again in my room. I whispered her name, "Alina". I stood, unaware of my nakedness, and ran to the back wall, away from the windows. I pounded my fists against it, screaming my dream's name, "ALINA!" The wall absorbed my fists, uttering a faint puff as it returned them unharmed. Eventually, I tired and fell against the wall, tears on my face.

Sliding down the wall until I was sitting, I reassembled the night before, tracing the memories carefully. As the sun neared its midday apex, I fell asleep curled against the wall, whispering her name.

A crash startled me awake. I look out the windows. The sun was low, it was dusk. I stood too quickly, nearly

Alone

collapsing as the blood rushed from my head. I grabbed my trousers on the way to the window. There I found the source of the noise. A large bird had flown into one of my windows, breaking its neck. It lay in a shattered heap on the ground below, barely breathing. I watched as it slowly died, helpless from inside my room, my prison.

Tomorrow the bird would be gone, as had all the others. And too, the cracked window, resembling a huge spider web, would be repaired. But for now, as the sun crept behind the horizon, I watched the web dance in colors of a prism, and thought of Alina.

But that was an eternity ago, and there has been many, many more unfortunate birds that I have watched die outside my windows. And there has been one change to my room. A change that keeps me awake at night, forbids me from dreaming of Alina. A change that haunts my thoughts, terrorizes my dreams and forces me to live in a constant nightmare. In the back, right corner, up high, is a spider web.

SmokeStone

    The morning is chilly near the ocean, the boatyard still asleep. The sun isn't up yet, and won't be for three more hours. I sit astride my 900 and look to the heavens. The sky is clear, the stars still bright in the pre-dawn hours. I'm about to leave on vacation. It had been six years since I went on a vacation. Most of my spare time and money goes into my dream of escape.

    I drop my gaze from the stars and looked at my sailboat sitting in her cradle. She has been sitting there for five years, slowly becoming a seaworthy vessel again. All the restoration has been done by me on weekends and five years of vacation time. She is a small schooner, thirty-two feet on deck, but she is my salvation. She is my escape.

    A labor of love, she's near completion now; the spar still needs to be installed and the sails put on board, but other than that, she's ready to be lifted back into the water. She had always motivated me, pushed me to keep going, keep working on her, no matter how hopeless it looked. Earlier this evening, after five years of anticipation, I painted her name on the stern - *MARY JANE*.

But I wanted her ready now. I wanted to be on her, NOW! Already out to sea and thousands of miles away. Instead my escape, my hope for tranquility in my life sits stoically, waiting for a few more years to pass to save enough money to sail away.

But I have to take a break. Six years is a long time to be in the city, even such a pretty one as San Diego; even though weekdays I stay in the cabin near the observatory where I work, I have to get away. What do they say, recharge my batteries. But it's more than that, more deeper. Deep into nature without interruptions. Recharge my soul. I need a break from civilization. Hell, that's my reason for wanting to sail away in the first place, to escape from the madness of civilization.

I turn away from Mary Jane and don my helmet equipped for sound, tightening the chin strap before turning over the motorcycle engine.

The 900 starts with a freshly tuned roar. I gun the throttle and adjust the choke, settling the engine into a smooth hum. I flip the lid to the CD player strapped to my belt and check the label. Confirming the artist, I close the lid and plug in power from the bike. I plug in the headphone cord coming from the helmet and down under my jacket. I watch the player as it goes through start-up, then program the three songs I want to hear, putting them on repeat.

Today I was taking off for three weeks of camping in

the remotes of an ancient forest. It was an eighteen hour ride.

The first song began to play and I lowered the volume so I could hear the engine. I checked the lights, using the mirrors to check for the glow behind me. I kicked up the sidestand, pulled in the clutch, downshifted to first gear and headed out the parking lot.

After the short drive up the gravel road from the docks, long enough to warm up the bike and the chilly air to thoroughly wake me up, I reached the city streets. The roads were nearly empty of traffic. I was tempted to turn up the CD and haul ass, but decided against it. I didn't want to start out my vacation with a speeding ticket. I was risking a ticket as it was with the songs I picked.

Three stoplights from the on-ramp, while waiting at a red, I reached to my side and turned the volume up. I increased it until I couldn't hear my engine.(I even gunned the throttle a few hundred RPM) The light turned green and I darted forward, the words of the song pounding into my head. Moments later, a few measures, I turned onto the freeway, going entirely too fast, headed north.

I signaled and checked behind me; clear. I angled to the fast lane. It would take me close to an hour to escape the city and all the surrounding towns. The traffic was heavier than the surface streets, but nothing to really concern myself with. I reached back with each leg and flicked down the passenger foot pegs. I hooked the heels of my boots onto the pegs and adjusted my seat, then adjusted my crotch. The song went instrumental and I increased speed, leaning forward a little more, balancing on the wind.

I increased speed a little more. I didn't notice, just

reacted by leaning forward a little more. The strong beat and steady guitar playing filled the space inside the helmet. For the time being, I was part of the road, the song, the bike. Visions inspired by a video game ran through my visor. My speed steadily increased until the tachometer was close to the red and the speedometer read 118. My mind had fallen into the rhythm of the music and the frequency of the bike. The city slipped by in a hazy blur. The cars I passed barely registered. A line, however, from the song did...

...where am I to go now that I've gone too far..?

I dropped my left hand from the handlebars and put it behind me, checking the gear secured to the seat before resting my hand on top of it. I was cruisin'.

The words returned in the song and started memories and thoughts of my own. The emotion of the song coming through in the beat. I drove. The words of the song lost in my reverie. The loneliness of my life forced before me.

The song changed. In the seconds of silence between songs I noticed my speed. I eased off the throttle, letting the bike slow to a cool seventy, rising as the wind decreased. I threatened myself to cut that song out of the programming if I couldn't keep the speed down.

I glanced around to make sure I was still on the proper freeway: I was, having made several interchanges. I was almost out of the city.

Another song started. The words and melody caused me to remember my past loves, shared and a cappella; all failures. I drove. The music, though still loud, was background to my thoughts. I drove by habit, by instinct. Perhaps I had envisioned too much with each one. Hoping each one could live up to the one I had dreamt of so many, many empty nights.

Yes, how many were there? Two wives, four girlfriends. I think. All of them failed relationships. I still can't understand, nor forget, the one night stand years ago back in Missouri. Arkansas? The best I can come up with was mutual curiosity.

But what of those I never told? Admiring quietly from a distance, some even with anonymous notes? Most of them were in the distant past, fifteen, twenty years ago. That's a long time to remember, dream about someone, but I have been alone for along time now and memories are all I have. Had I ever really known love?

The sudden washing of pink on the eastern sky jerked me from my absorption of old flames and fantasies. I was doing 125 this time. I was also out of the city. The song ended,

...Where am I to go now that I've gone too far..?

then restarted. I pulled over onto the shoulder and stopped, placing the bike in neutral. I unhooked the CD player from my belt and looked at the display. It was on one song repeat. I checked my watch. Two hours had passed. It was time for petrol.

I was headed for the high mountains and deep forest of the Sierra Nevada's. I knew of a place near Sherman Peak where I could finish stripping off layers of city that the ride will have started. I was going to survive off what I had on the motorcycle, which wasn't much, and the land.

But that's the way I wanted it. The way it used to be two centuries ago. Out in the wilderness, where it was me and Mother Nature. 'Cept I was going to live with Nature, not against her. The tranquility that overcomes me when I'm with

Nature the city has no match for. It's almost as if I become part of the environment, hearing and sensing things that I can't in the city. I feel alive, all my senses on.

That's why I live near my work, Mount Palomar Observatory; it keeps me out of the city except for weekends, and then I'm down with my boat at the marina. I am a junior astronomer at Palomar and had been given permission by the Forestry Service to occupy a small cabin that had been used by rangers some years ago. It was a fifteen minute walk from the observatory.

I pulled off the freeway and into a fueling station. I filled the tank, then paid the attendant. The stop lasted five minutes.

Back on the freeway, as I hooked my heels on the rear foot pegs, I realized why the attendant stared at me like he had; I never shut off the CD player. I had only reprogrammed the songs.

So too, my thoughts hadn't quit. It had also dawned on me that morning that one of the reasons I became an astronomer was because I could never fit the nine-to-five routine; nor the ties. Life seemed so artificial that way, so man-made. Besides, my biological clock made me nocturnal. I reached down and turned up the volume a little more. I was cruisin' again. And lucky. I didn't get a single ticket on the way to Sherman Peak.

Chapter 2

It was on the third day of camping that I was attacked. The remote spot I had so carefully picked, the beauty of the trees, the serenity of the hills, the quiet, all were ruptured by an ambush.

It was an hour or so past noon. I had been in my tent rolling a joint when I heard voices a short distance away.

Nobody knew where I was, not even the park rangers. There is only one reason to come way out here: they had followed me. They didn't know how close they were to my camp, or didn't care. The "illegal" paranoia instilled by the surprise visit had my stash hidden in half a minute. I moved to exit the tent, then paused by the opening, listening. I could hear their footfalls and what they were saying now. It was too late, I was stuck in the tent.

"Remember, they want him alive. Don't kill this one." His voice was low, deep.

"Give it a rest. I said I was sorry. Besides, like I said, he pissed me off." His voice was grating, a forced toughness.

"Just control yourself."

"Piss off!"

"Sh! I can see a tent."

Suddenly an idea hit. I began to snore, softly.

I heard them creep up to the side of the tent as I looked around for a weapon with only my eyes, scared to even turn my head. I remembered the hunting knife on my belt. I unsheathed it as the deeper voice spoke. They were right outside and I choked back a whimper to sound like a snore.

"See. Ya' woke 'im."

"Did no.."

"Shhh!"

I waited a moment more, listening for more footsteps. There were only the two. I moved as quietly as possible, getting off my knees and crouched onto my feet. I moaned, part to play the scene of rolling over, part to answer my screaming knees.

"See, he's stil.."

"Shhhh! The fire's g.."

I leaped towards them through the tent, intent on 'netting' them with it. I draped the three of us with the tent and we fell to the ground, me on top.

I felt the knife go into something soft. From the groan I surmised it was the one with the deep voice. I suddenly felt sick.

This is not what I had planned. The canvas darkened, the dark spot growing outward from the knife. I withdrew my knife from the lifeless body. I was angry, almost in a rage for having killed a man. I took my anger out on the other lump beneath the canvas. I started prodding, demanding answers.

"What do you want!!?" I screamed. No answer. Poke. Poke. "What the fuck do you want!?!" Poke. Poke.

BANG!!!

I saw the muzzle blast burst through the canvas. It was as the hot metal grazed my left temple that I plunged the knife into the other lump beneath the tent, repeatedly.

...where am I to go now that I've gone too far..?

I crawled out from beneath the tent and pulled the bloodied canvas off the two dead bodies. These were my first dead bodies. They were also my first murders. No. It was self-defense. But, I had killed them! I vomited until I was heaving up nothing but air.

I wiped my mouth with my sleeve and searched their pockets. My head hurt where the bullet nicked me, but I had to know who they were and why they wanted me.

They wore dark suits and had close cropped hair. My search revealed a wad of twenties on both men and pistols. Nothing as to who they were nor what they wanted. I still had no idea what was going on.

I bandaged the wound on my head, deciding to find my stash in the mess we had made and finish rolling a joint. Then I would figure out what to do next.

With the joint rolled and lit, I sat back against a fallen tree and stared at the corpses in my campsite. I knew I had to go the police, but finding no identification on the bodies concerned me. Who were they and what did they want with me? I'm an astronomer. What could I know, or have, that anybody would want to kidnap me for?

As I climbed through the purple cloud I scanned my past for a hint to why this happened. I went back through the misdirected loves, the schools, the menial jobs while I went through school. Nothing. Nothing in my past could I find to warrant what had just happened. What did I know?

I went through my current life, over my weekly routine and still came up with nothing. I did very little on the Internet outside of research. I do play Cycle Sin, a video game for the television. Three nights a week the Professor and I play it as the computer tracks the sky. I rent it from the video store. I only talk to one person down at the boatyard, and then we only talk about our boats. I spend most of my nights at the observatory, my days sleeping. Weekends are spent with my boat. I don't give the Professor any grief...

I heard a stick break. Someone was coming from the same direction as the other two. I threw the joint into the fire and crawled over to the corpses. I pulled the pistol from the bigger one's hand and the extra clip from his waist, then slid into the bushes and waited.

Moments later I heard someone talking. Another criminal.

"I told them they wanted them alive. If they've killed another one..." One man entered the campsite and abruptly stopped. He had been talking to himself. He stared at the bodies, then quickly studied the campsite. I held my breath. He looked back at the corpses.

He had not seen me. I, however, could see him.

He was in a business suit. I guessed his age in his thirties, maybe late twenties. He was white. His flat-top haircut causing him to look like a Marine. He lit a cigarette, then pulled out a cellular phone. He pushed a button then held it to his ear.

"Williams here. Two of my Recruiters are dead."

Pause.

"Yes sir."

Another pause as Williams scanned the area. "No sir, I don't see him."

Pause.

"Yes sir, I'll wait." Williams turned off the cellular phone and placed it back in his pocket.

Wait!?! For who? Back up? Me to return to the scene of my crime? I raised the pistol, aimed, swallowed, then pulled the trigger. A small, high-pitched explosion broke the wild silence. Williams stumbled back and fell over his Recruiters, his abdomen turning red.

I waited several seconds before moving, the pistol still aimed in his direction. Williams didn't move. I broke from the bushes and ran to him. He was pale and wasn't breathing.

Great. Three dead men at my hands. I was near panic.

"What have I done?!?" I screamed under my breath. And what was I to do? I backed away from the corpses and headed for the mess that was once my serene camp.

I quickly packed what little I could think of to pack, stuffing things into the bag on the motorcycle's gas tank and my backpack. I put on my jacket, stuffing the pistol into the back of my pants, and mounted the 900. I left the helmet on the sissy bar, wanting to hear anything I could; approaching cars, helicopters, anything. Plus, my head hurt. I put on my sunglasses and started the bike.

I let the engine warm up as I sat there and trembled. I had just killed three men. I was about ready to flee the scene of the crime.

...where am I to go now that I've gone too far...?

More were coming. Williams was going to wait all right. He'll be there, waiting. I put the bike in first and started out of the forest. I was headed east, yet I rode without direction, just out of the forest. Before I reached the highway I had decided not to go home. Whomever "They" were would be there waiting, watching.

Chapter 3

I pulled onto Highway 395 just after leaving the forest and went North. The afternoon was turning into evening. My helmet was on, so too, the CD player. I was cruisin'. Only this time I knew full well how fast I was going - not fast enough! I checked my mirrors again. No one behind me. So far so good. My head still ached where the bullet grazed my temple, but it had stopped bleeding before I left the forest and was scabbing over nicely.

When Highway 190 popped up a some minutes later, I stopped at the intersection and looked behind me. No one. No one following me, nor any other traffic. It had been like that since getting on the highway. Something wasn't right. Where were the police? Where were the road blocks; the helicopters? I had killed three men. Where was the man-hunt?!

I looked west and absorbed the sunset. The sun was an hour away from the mountains, the clouds beginning to turn pink. It would be getting chilly soon. I turned on the 190 the only way I could, East.

Twenty minutes had passed when I made the turn to Darwin. I needed petrol. It was a long way across Death Valley.

After I had filled the tank and paid the attendant, I put on two layers of shirts under my jacket, re-stuffing the pistol in the back of my pants before getting back on my motorcycle.

Just as I sat on the bike, a man in a business suit stepped out from behind the gas station. This man, too, had a flat-top.

I looked in the windows of the building. The station attendant had conveniently disappeared.

I quickly put on my helmet, not bothering to cinch it down, and started the bike. The man in the suit started running towards me, shouting that I "hold up". I gunned the throttle and released the clutch. The back tire squealed, then caught. I raced out the gas station driveway pushing the front end down.

I looked back at the station after getting on the road. The man in the suit was running back behind the building. A moment later a car was vibrating in my mirrors. I took the first right, pulling onto a dirt road.

The sun was behind the mountains now and it wouldn't be long before it was black out. I reached down and unplugged the brake light switch for the foot pedal, then did the same for the hand lever. I prayed to anybody's god, then turned off my headlight.

Car headlights pulled in behind me minutes later. At least the dirt road was flat and thus far, free of gullies and potholes. I downshifted and gave the bike throttle. I glanced quickly at the speedometer. It read 85 MPH. I was going to kill myself.

The headlights in my mirrors receded. I slowed down and plugged in my helmet, then hit the power switch on the CD player. As the song started, I eased open the throttle. I fell into the beat of the song. I checked the speedometer. 90MPH. Game time.

Some minutes later, before the first song ended, I slowed down. I reached behind me and pulled the pistol out from the back of my pants. I released the safety, then stuffed the pistol down the front of my pants.

I slid the bike off the road and into the ditch, then back towards the car, keeping my head and speed down. I stopped when the car was close. It raced by me doing about fifty.

I pulled back onto the road behind him, my headlight still off, and chased him down. When I was close enough so I shouldn't miss, I pulled out the pistol and aimed at his rear tire. It took two bullets to hit the back tire on the passenger side.

The car swerved to the right. The driver compensated and the car fishtailed back to the left, then right, left, right and dove into the ditch.

I slowed, putting the pistol back in my pants behind me as I passed the car in the ditch. I could see the driver moving. I flicked on the headlights then twisted the throttle and sped away, thankful I hadn't killed this man, too.

When the dirt road became rough sometime later I had to slow down. I had been kicking up dust for half an hour now, the 90 MPH having been dropped to a slow forty long ago. It was time to see where I was going. I stopped at an outcropping of rocks, pulling behind them and out of sight of what was left of the road.

I pulled out a flashlight and checked my watch. It had been an hour since I stopped to get gas. The desert was black. I switched off the flashlight. The waxing crescent moon would be up in a couple hours. I removed my helmet and looked around. I couldn't see any lights anywhere. Calm returned to my breathing. I put the bike on the center-stand and climbed atop the rocks.

I could see the silhouette of the horizon, the view panoramic; to the southeast a tall peak. The wind filled my ears with their whispers. The night was beautiful, yet I couldn't enjoy it. Killing those three men had changed me. Even though it was self-defense, I had learned when I was young how precious and fragile life is; a close uncle had been killed in a car crash when I was twelve.

I climbed down the rocks and pulled out my map and leather chaps from the bag on the gas tank. If there was a way through the Amargossa range other than Highway 178, I was going to find it.

According to the map the peak to the southeast was Funeral Peak. My goal was Pahrump, home of the Martian invasion of 1996. I had been there a number of times and knew of an abandoned observatory in the area. I stowed the map and flashlight, then put on my chaps and another shirt. It was going to get chilly and I was going to off-road it for a while.

I secured my helmet to the sissy bar, then put on a skull cap and goggles. I checked behind me for headlights before starting the motorcycle.

Ten minutes later I crossed Highway 178 at a bend, headed for a gap to the south of Funeral Peak. As I shifted up to third, a semi-truck raced north on the 178 behind me. It was the first vehicle I had seen other than the dark car at the gas station in Darwin.

I picked my way across the desert, riding most the time standing with bent knees on the foot pegs

The gap in the mountains widened as I slowly approached. I still couldn't figure out why anyone would want me. Had I perhaps seen something at the observatory? I had to get answers. Somehow, I had to get answers.

I worried about the truck that could have seen my headlight until I reached the foothills of the Amargossa mountains. The moon was up and I was heading right for it. It wasn't going to be bright enough for me to run without my headlight as I crossed the mountains, but I had my hopes up for the flat on the other side.

I found a service road that was more like a path, about a mile from the gap. It was better than picking my way through the open desert, but the gullies left by the rains was beating the crap out of me and the bike.

An hour later I had my helmet back on, the CD blaring through the little speakers. I was running fast on the flat on the other side of the mountain on a southeast course. The lights were off as I rode in the loom of the moon.

I don't remember ever feeling that exhilarated, racing across the charcoal grey desert. I felt alive and so in tune with Nature that I swear I could feel the cacti and shrubbery ahead of me, avoiding them without really seeing them. I was in the video game, Cycle Sin, the pulse of the rock beat in my ears confirming the situation.

When I came across pavement I stopped and plugged

in all the lights, then headed south to a junction. I had to pull into the first gas station that was open.

                *   *   *

"He killed both Recruiters; Thompson and Grant, and wounded Williams."

"Where is he?"

"He's been spotted on the 178, headed south. He's cutting through the desert. Looks like he's headed for Pahrump."

"Get men there."

"On their way, sir."

Chapter 4

Dawn awoke the windblown clouds with shades of red. I rounded a bend and Pahrump spread out ahead. I stopped at the first gas station, a convenience store. I topped off the gas tank and picked up some canned tuna and jerky.

Still on the outskirts of Pahrump, I stopped at a cafe to eat and find out what I could about what was happening. I picked up a newspaper before entering the cafe.

The cafe was small, a counter spanned ten tables, five on either side of the door, all of them empty. I took the second one down on my left, putting my helmet on the table. The cycle sat outside the window. I ordered oatmeal and toast when the waitress arrived. She was cute, a little young, but still cute.

I unfolded the paper and scanned the headlines after watching her walk away. There was no mention of the deaths back at Sherman Peak. I put it off to Pahrump being a small town, then smiled at the waitress as she passed by. She smiled back. Genuine, I hoped.

What was I thinking? I was on the run from someone. And she was probably a PYTBULL - Pretty Young Thing But Under Legal Limit.

When she came up from behind and spoke to me moments later, I nearly jumped off the bench seat.

"I'll go get your order now," she said.

I watched her walk away, shameless in my thoughts. Her narrow body swayed in youthful rhythm. I turned to the paper, searching for the comics.

The waitress returned a minute later with my order. She set it in front of me, touched me on the shoulder and said,

"I'll be right back."

She left before I could respond, although I don't know what I would have said. I put several pats of butter on the oatmeal then smothered it with sugar. I dug in with the soup spoon, the comic section in hand. The waitress returned before I had my third bite.

"Hi," she said as she sat down across from me. "How's the oatmeal?"

"Fine."

"You ride a motorcycle, don't you?"

I looked at my helmet on the table, then at my cycle outside, then at the waitress. Her eyes were a clear green, her nose short and wide, mouth thin. Her light, brown hair was spun up in a mass on her head. I nodded.

She looked out the window. "Foreign, hunh?"

I nodded again. I was still stunned at her boldness. I wondered if she did this with everyone. "So, do you provide company and conversation for all the diners," I glanced at her nameplate, "Rachel?"

"No. Just the good looking spies who ride motorcycles."

I almost spat a mouthful of oatmeal at her. I grabbed the water and quickly washed down the food. Those moments of forced hesitation kept me from screaming, 'Spy?!'. Instead I said, "What makes you think I'm a spy?"

"The government agents that were in here last night. Said we were to report you if we saw ya'."

I nearly jumped from the seat. I took a bite of toast, then asked, "FBI?"

Rachel shrugged. "They flashed their badges too fast. I did see federal something, though. They were talking with Clem."

"Clem?"

"He owns this rat hole. Cooks the oatmeal, too."

"You going to report me, or did you already?"

"No. Clem wanted to when you walked in. Thought you were who those men were looking for, but I told him you were an old flame of mine."

I stared at her in disbelief. "Why?"

"First you gotta tell me. Are you the one they're looking for?"

My mind went into a spin I had no control over. Do I tell her the truth, or try to lie? Was she the waitress, or with Them? What the HELL did I do?

I decided not to lie; I have never been very good at lying. Hell, I've never been good with people. Besides, something told me I could trust her. Maybe it was her eyes. Their clear green colour allowed me in. I wondered what made her think she could trust me. "What did they say I did?"

"They say you killed two of their men that were trying to bring you in for software piracy."

Two? Who isn't dead? Williams? One of the Recruiters? "It was self-defense. And I don't know anything about stealing any software." I dropped my eyes to the table. "I'm not a spy. I'm an astronomer."

I looked up and around the cafe. Rachel and I were alone, Clem having never left the back. I looked back at Rachel. "I have no idea what's going on. Only that I'm running from somebody."

"What's your name?" Rachel asked me.

"Stone."

"Stone? Just Stone? No first name, or is that your first name?"

"It's a nickname." I looked outside, back down the highway. It was still clear. Maybe I had gotten away. Maybe not. Either way, I had to get going.

"Why won't you tell me your name?"

I looked at her. "I did."

"Those government guys wouldn't tell us your name, either. I didn't like them."

"But you like me?"

"I've always had a soft spot for bikers. Don't suppose I could come with you, hunh?"

I looked at her with disbelief. "You suppose right. How old are you?" I was expecting her to say she had another year of high school.

"I'm twenty-two. Be twenty-three in a month. I'm so sick of this place. Nothing ever happens. My Aunt is in a home now and I'm itching to get out of this trailer stricken town."

I liked the town.(...I've always been partial to small towns...) I had fourteen years on her. I was also on the run. "How much do I owe you for the oatmeal?"

"Free, if you take me with you."

"That wouldn't be a good idea, Rachel. I don't know what's waiting for me. I don't even know what I've done. And," I looked into her eyes, wanting to get to know her, "I don't know you. You're better off sitting here bored. How much?"

"Three seventy-five," she said with a huff.

I slid off the seat and stood, digging in my front pants pocket for money. I handed her a five. "Keep the change."

"Ooh, now I can buy a car and get away on my own."

"There's an idea." I grabbed my helmet and headed for the door as she went to the cash register.

Outside, the sun was still in early climb mode, singeing the clouds with gold and pulling in shadows. A car was coming from the east. It was miles away, but it gave me an uneasy feeling. I knew it was them. She did call. I straddled the 900.

"Hi."

I jumped, fumbling with my helmet, almost dropping it. I hadn't seen, nor heard Rachel approach. She stood to my left.

"Didn't mean to scare you. But I thought I better tell you that Clem called those men that were looking for you. Said he called them when you buying the paper."

Damn. I looked in her eyes. She had such pretty eyes. I didn't think she was lying. "Thanks."

I looked down the road. The car was getting closer. "I better go." I slid on the helmet and started the bike. Rachel plopped down behind me.

"Hey!?! Off!" I screamed inside the helmet.

"No."

...falling down a spiral, destination unknown...

The car was getting real close. They must be doing over to a hundred.

"OFF!!!"

She put her arms around me and squeezed, pressing the backpack into her and the pistol into me. I twisted to make her let go, then took off my helmet.

"Rachel, you need to get off. This isn't a game." I was talking fast and loud. "These men want me for something that I know nothing about. Their tactics so far indicate I'll be forced at whatever it is they want me to do. You don't want to come with me." I emphasized 'don't'.

"Yes, I do. You'll get away. Just like the movies."

I could hear the engine of the approaching car, it was screaming. There was no more time to argue with *the movies*. I just hoped she was right. Rachel, the waitress, was coming with me. At least for a short time.

"Here", I said, handing her my only helmet, "you get to wear the brain bucket. I wanna' catch bugs in my teeth. That oatmeal just wasn't enough."

"That's sick."

I pulled the backpack from between us and handed it to her. "You also get to wear this."

"Thanks."

"None necessary. Just hurry." I pulled the clear goggles and skull cap from the pack on the tank.

She hefted the straps over her shoulders and continued

fastening the helmet.

"You ever ridden one of these before?" I asked her as I checked her chin strap.

"Uh..", she shook her head.

"Hold on to me tight and lean with me."

She nodded, then grabbed me around the waist again and pulled tight. When she felt the bulge of the pistol, she eased off her grip, hesitated, then held me a little looser. I could see details on the car now, and the three silhouettes inside. I put the bike in gear.

"Ready?"

A muffled, "Yes", came out of the helmet.

Rachel coming along was not a good idea. I didn't like it. Neither her nor I knew what she was getting herself into. I eased out the clutch and headed for the car, hating myself for not pushing Rachel off the bike. *...what if she's one of Them..?*

About forty miles south of Pahrump was an abandoned observatory at Kingston Peak. There was a service road a few miles ahead that led to it. If I could loose the G-men I could think things through there, figure out what do to with Rachel.

The car had slowed down when we got on the road. I leaned forward and twisted the throttle. The bike hardly noticed the extra weight. I did though. I shifted in the red each time and was doing just over a ninety when we passed them. I checked my mirrors after passing them. The car turned around in a cloud of dust and grey smoke from spinning tires. I tapped Rachel on the knee and leaned forward until my chest rested on the pack lashed to the gas tank. Rachel followed me down. In moments we were at a hundred miles per hour, now inside Pahrump city limits. I felt her squeeze tighter while our speed increased. I tapped the back of her hands when it became difficult to breathe. The song from the CD began to play in my head. We were cruisin'.

Rachel stuffed her hands in my jacket pockets. I remembered not seeing a jacket on her at the cafe's parking lot. I glanced down at her arms around my waist and saw she was wearing a sweatshirt. Her bare legs, though, were turning pink in the cold morning air.

We came to the top of a rise and I saw the turn-off for the service road up ahead. I checked the mirrors, then cranked my head to the rear. It was going to be close. I wished it were night. As we zoomed down the incline, I tapped Rachel's arm and pointed to the right. On the horizon were mountains. I pointed to them, trying to indicate that that is where we were headed. She gave me a thumbs up. I wondered if she understood.

The service road was at the bottom of the grade. Five hundred feet away I hit both brakes, hard. The back tire locked up and I eased off the pedal. I didn't want to give them warning. We ended up sliding by the road, causing us to backtrack and lose time.

The south side, the side we wanted, was gated. The road was paved as far as I could see. Maybe the gate would buy me some time and I could get rid of my passenger.

Rachel pushed open the locked chainlink gate as far as it would go against the chain and padlock. With me pushing and twisting the bike, we managed to squeeze through.

As I waited for Rachel to make her way through the gate, I was tempted to take off without her, but the men in the car would see her and know which way I went. I was stuck with her. And just what would they have done to her?

Rachel climbed on behind me and stuffed her hands in my jacket pockets again. We took off fast, me checking the highway as I shifted up. There was a rise ahead with rocks that would hide us from the road. I felt panic rise in my gut, afraid we would be seen before we made it there and the chase would be on. As it was, they were sure to be on our trail in hours. But I was sure I could lose them in the desert.

I glanced back to the highway as we neared the top of the hill. I could see their car. It was slowing.

I hit the brakes as we crested the rise, the back end fishtailing. I heard Rachel scream. I unlocked the rear wheel and downshifted. When we were slow enough, I turned back around and headed for the rocks just this side of the crest. I stopped the bike and told Rachel to get off. I then dismounted and laid the 900 down on its side, hiding it completely. I had an idea.

"Hide behind the rocks," I ordered Rachel.

"What are we doing?"

"They saw us. I have to stop them. I have to get some answers."

"How do you plan on that?"

"You'll see. Now be quiet."

The car was approaching fast. I was impressed with the sound of the engine. As it climbed the hill nearing us, I stretched out prone along side a large rock. Sliding up so I could see the road, I aimed the pistol at where I thought the front tire would be when they topped the hill. I waited only seconds, but it seemed an eternity as the possibilities of the aftermath raced through my mind.

The roar of the engine intensified quickly, then suddenly there it was. The tire was in the gun sight. I jerked the trigger, seeing a puff of dust on the spinning tire. The car was in the air now, sailing hundreds of feet down the hill.

...Christ! they jumped the hill...they're going to have a bad landing...

I sat up against the rock and watched, horrified, as the car came down and lurched to the right: the side I shot out the front tire. The car then whipped to the left for just a moment before whipping back to the right and begin to flip. It did the bumper dance and the driver's door roll before coming to rest at the bottom of the long hill in the ditch on the far side.

"You okay, Stone?"

I turned from the wreck to Rachel. "Just shaken up. I'm fine." I dusted myself off. "You wait here, I'll be right back." I stuffed the pistol in the back of my pants and picked up the bike. Rachel said something as I started the bike, but I lost it in the sound of the engine and drove off, ignoring her.

I watched the odometer as I raced to the wreck, hoping one of them would be alive. I didn't allow myself to think about the possibility of more deaths, I just assumed it. I hit the brakes, checking the distance as I skidded to a halt. They had rolled in the car for about a thousand feet. My hopes for answers sunk. I kicked out the side-stand and killed the engine.

The car had stopped upside down, nose to the road. The front tire on the driver's side spinning freely. I could hear but not see flames. I assumed the engine was on fire. I stepped towards the car, pulling out the pistol from my back, and knelt by the back window, the widest opening.

"Anybody alive?" I shouted in.

The man in the back moaned. I crawled in as far as I could, barely getting my shoulders in. I stretched to touch his shoulder.

"Who are you, and why do you want me?" I questioned him.

"Get me outta here," his voice was low, forced.

"I'll pull you clear after you give me some answers."

"There isn't time! It's gonna blow!"

"And you with it. Now tell me what I want to know!"

"Fuck you."

"Fine." I started backing out.

"Wait! You gotta pull me out!"

"No. I don't." I couldn't believe how cold I was, yet, I hadn't looked in the front seat. I took my first step away from the car and the man inside screamed,

"They want you because of your high scores!"

I nearly dove back into the car. The smell of the fire was getting strong. "What?!? High scores!? What are you talking about?"

"You gotta pull me out now, Smokestone! NOW!!"

"Tell me who and what for!!"

"PULL ME OUT!!!"

"WHAT FOR!!!"

"To fly missiles!!! Now get me the fuck outta here!!!"

I tried to grab his shirt, but he was just too far away. I backed out and ran around to the other side, the entire time the man in the car screaming at me to "Come back".

The car was smashed on this side, the windows but slits. I could see the soles of his feet and his butt through the slit. I ran back to the other side and pulled on the door. It didn't make a sound. I crawled back inside the car.

"I..I'm sorry. I can't get you out. The other side is smashed. I can't get in any further. I can't get the door open," I felt tears begin to rise. I squeezed my eyes shut to push them back. "I can't get you out. Can you move at all?" I looked at him, into his eyes. He was terrified. He didn't want to die. Then I did it. I looked in the front seat.

The two men were dead. The driver was impaled on the steering wheel, the passenger with blood all over his head.

"I'm sorry about your comrades. You guys were going pretty fast."

"I can't move anything. I'm pinned."

A small explosion from the engine compartment rocked the car.

"Carburetor," he said.

"She's gonna blow," I said matter-of-factly.

"Uh, yea." He looked at the two in the front seat, then back at me. "Uh, could you do me a favor, Smokestone?"

I had a bad feeling. "Make it Stone."

"Shoot me before the car explodes. Could you do that for me, Stone?" He looked away. I saw his body jerk. He was crying.

"What's your name?" I choked out.

"Jerry." He looked at me, tears pouring out of his eyes. "Will you?" He looked away. "Will you? I don't want to burn alive."

I pointed the pistol at the top of his head, then pulled the trigger. His blood squirted on my arm, shoulder, ...*where am I to go now that I've gone too far..?* and the right side of my face. I left a trail of vomit as I pushed myself out of the car with one stroke.

I ran to my bike, starting it as I hit the seat, kicking up the side-stand on the bounce. I gunned the throttle and released the clutch, cutting an arc in the sand as I took off back to Rachel. The car exploded halfway to Rachel.

Rachel's face drained of colour when she saw me. The blood on me was beginning to dry, becoming sticky. I thought she was going to faint.

"You shot 'em?!"

I turned off the engine and set the bike on the side-stand. "Him. I had no choice." I looked to the ground, not wanting to see his face again. "He was trapped and.." I walked past her and fell beside a rock.

Five, now. Five men I've killed. And why? Why?!? Because they wanted me to fly missiles?! How did playing Cycle Sin qualify me to fly missiles? And who were "They"? I rocked onto my knees and screamed in desperation, frustration over events I have had little control over. In the solitude out there in the desert, with only the wind and the burning flames, my scream filled the air. I formed no words. The scream was primeval.

When I stopped, I looked at my right arm. It was red with blood. I grabbed a handful of sand and began scrubbing off the blood. Rachel came towards me then.

"Stone?" She was hesitant. "Are you okay?"

"No. I'm not." I continued scrubbing. "I've killed five men now. All because they want me to fly missiles. I don't know how to fly missiles. Five men. Five men.." I scrubbed.

"Stone?" Rachel stepped closer. "Stone? Are you going to be all right?" She touched me on the shoulder and I broke into tears. She sat down and pulled me to her.

I cried on her for ten minutes, for an eternity, not near long enough, jerking us both with my sobs. When I pulled away from the front of her shoulder, I strung mucus from my nose to her shirt. It snapped and hit me in the mouth. I wiped my sleeve across my lips and stood up.

"We need to get going. I want to make the observatory before dark." I was embarrassed for breaking down; for turning to her for strength. I kept talking to void the memory. I filled her in on my plan to turn east ten miles up, then find a ravine to backtrack in. I wanted to make them think we were headed to Las Vegas. The detour is what would put us at the observatory late. I also warned her that there was going to be a lot of off-road travel.

She asked again about the shooting at the car as we walked to the bike, but I put her off with a wave of my hand. I had told her enough. I was trying unsuccessfully to put it out of my mind. I gave her my chaps to put on before mounting the 900.

We had to pull off the pavement to pass the flames. Flashes of the moment I pulled the trigger on the man inside flipped through my mind like pages from a Stephen King novel. I gave the engine throttle and we shot back onto the road. A half-mile further the road turned to dirt.

Chapter 5

I stopped the bike in front of the observatory. It looked like a sugar cube with a dome on top. Rachel dismounted. We had made good time and had about two hours worth of daylight left. I pushed the bike between the bushes and the stairs.

"It doesn't look finished", Rachel said as she looked at the structure. Although the doors were installed, most of the windows were boarded up. The concrete was unpainted and the grounds had not been prepared.

"It isn't", came my voice from the bushes. After no more information was offered, she spoke again.

"How come?"

Silence again. As she moved closer to repeat the question, I emerged from the bushes. She stepped back, a little startled.

"They started building it in 'thirty-seven." I explained as we walked to the door. "When Hitler started invading

Europe two years later they stopped work on it. I'm pretty sure they don't know about it, though."

"What makes you so sure they don't know about it?"

"Give me a second and I'll show you." I turned my attention to the door.

They were heavy, wooden double doors; the main entrance. One side had been locked to the floor and to the top of the jam on the inside. On my first visit two decades ago, I broke in one of the few windows and unlocked the bolts. Now all I needed to do was pull - hard.

The doors snapped open, sending me backpedaling several steps into Rachel. We stood there several moments in each others grasp, neither of us sure what to do. Finally I said, "Let's go inside." We picked up the bags and entered the unfinished observatory.

"See," I said, nodding my head towards the center of the room. Rachel looked in the direction indicated. The room was round. No interior walls had been installed and she could see the other side of the building. In the middle, however, was the telescope.

"They left the telescope," I said. "They wouldn't leave that if they hadn't forget about this place," I challenged.

"You have a point. But, how do you know so much about it?"

"I found some paperwork, calendars, and newspapers. The newspapers were talking about Hitler's invasion of Poland."

"Does it work?" Rachel said, staring at the telescope.

"Sure does. I'll show you tonight."

"I'd like that."

"C'mon. Let's pick a place to bed down in."

I looked around the room. It had been over ten years since I had been here. On the south side a wood burning stove was near a window with a pane. I had moved the stove there and slept near it to stay warm.

"I'll see if I can get that stove working and we can sleep next to it to keep warm."

"Don't you get it, Motorcycle Man? I want you to keep me warm."

I looked into the young woman's eyes. Why did she want me? Just because I rode a motorcycle? Did she really believe me; in me? "I'd like that."

We put the bags by the stove and went outside through the south door.

"You gather firewood and I'll see if I can find something to eat." I pulled the pistol from my back.

Rachel looked around, then looked back at me. "Where do you suggest I find this wood?"

"You can find twigs and sometimes branches around the bushes. And if you go west you'll find the remains of a dead forest."

"You gonna be gone long?"

I looked towards the setting sun. "I hope not." Then I started down the slope.

When I returned with some roots and a skinny rabbit, the sun was kissing the dark ridges on the horizon goodnight. I could see Rachel had the fire going and the stove hot by the thin smoke from the smokestack. I skinned and cleaned the rabbit outside before announcing my arrival.

Inside, I put the roots and meat on the table by the

stove and grabbed the tank bag, noticing that Rachel had found and lit several candles. I dug out the mess kit and went out the west door to get some water. Rachel yelled after me asking how we were going to cook the rabbit.

"On the stove!" I yelled back.

As we waited for the rabbit to cook, Rachel told me a little about herself. We had put a blanket near the stove and candles surrounded the blanket.

"Dad worked at Groom Lake until just a few years ago. He and Mom were killed in a car wreck. I was seventeen. That's when I went to live with Aunt Toni."

"What did your father do at Groom Lake?" I had heard about Groom Lake, a.k.a. Area 51. It was top secret. All I knew about was the name.

Rachel shrugged. "I dunno. He couldn't talk about it."

"What kind of work did he do before working there?"

"He was an aeronautical engineer. Mom told me that they used to live in California. Pasadena. Mom was pregnant with me when they moved to Las Vegas."

She looked down, talking to the table as she went on. "Dad had gotten sick. I overheard him and Mom the night before the accident. They weren't arguing, but they were scared."

"Of what?"

She looked at me now. Into my eyes. "Of what the government would do if they found out that Dad was going to go to an outside doctor. That's where they were going when," she paused, holding back tears. "When they crashed."

"Crashed?" I queried.

"The sheriff's said they lost control of the car and went

off the road. He had said the skid marks indicated they swerved to miss something.

"I went to live with Aunt Toni in Pahrump after the funeral." She produced a small smile. "She's a lesbian," she stated, then giggled. "I think its kinda cute."

I smiled back.

"I went back to 'Vegas when I was twenty-one and became a dealer until Aunt Toni took ill. That was four months ago."

"Don't you feel like you ran out on her just now?" I asked.

"No, I don't. I told you, she's in a home. She has lots of friends there."

"But none of them are the niece she raised."

Rachel got up and checked the rabbit. She started talking without turning around, speaking to the rabbit. "I was going stir crazy there, Stone. Aunt Toni isn't around anymore to keep me company. None of the men there in that dusty little town interest me. They're all rednecks." She turned around and came towards me, kneeling in front of me. "Aunt Toni doesn't recognize me anymore, Stone. Do you know how much that hurts?"

"You know she can't help it."

"I know." Rachel leaned to me, her head down. I pulled her in as she began to sob. She rested her head on my chest.

I held her for several minutes as I watched the side of the rabbit blacken. I gently pushed her away.

"Dinner's burning." I stood as she rolled onto her butt.

"I'm sorry," she sobbed. "I didn't mean to ruin dinner."

"It's not ruined." I removed the rabbit from the heat,

setting it beside the cooked roots on the table.

"I try not to think about her, Aunt Toni, you know. But I needed to get it out."

I stayed where I was, fidgeting with fixing a plate. I was barely controlling myself from a screaming panic. My world was in disarray. Being at the observatory helped ease my nerves, but not much. What the man in the car said didn't make any sense. Fly missiles? That scene from the movie with Slim Pickens riding a nuke came to mind. It was ludicrous.

"I only play one game, and it's a motorcycle game. I don't know anything about flying a missile. I don't understand what's going on." I looked at her, into her eyes. "I don't understand you."

She stared back into me, then shrugged and whispered, "Destiny."

"That doesn't explain why you jumped on my motorcycle this morning."

"I don't trust the government anymore, Stone. Not after what happened with my parents. And when they came looking for you last night, and then I saw you this morning, I knew they were up to no good again. As for jumping on your bike.." she shrugged.

I looked into her eyes, looking for deceit. I couldn't see any. "Right. Come on and eat. It's ready."

As Rachel walked over she asked, "Is that what the guy in the car said? They want you to fly missiles"

Blood squirted onto my arm and shoulder from the wound I put in his head.

I closed my eyes and forced the bite of rabbit down my throat. "Yes."

"Why'd you shoot him?"

I heard him screaming as he burned this time, then heard him ask me to shoot him. "Because I couldn't pull him out," I said to the plate of food. I had lost my appetite.

Rachel came up behind me and put her arms around my waist as if we were on the motorcycle. She pulled herself close and whispered in my ear,

"I'm sorry, Motorcycle Man. I should have known by your eyes that you're not ruthless. Forgive me."

I turned in her arms to face her. "Forgive you for what?"

She looked into my eyes. "For doubting you."

It was then we kissed. A peck. Short and sweet. Oh how sweet were her lips. I was in trouble.

I gently pushed her away and described my boat to Rachel as we ate. I told her of my dream of sailing away. I told her my dream of owning this observatory. I told her my ideas of wormholes and dark matter. I told her too many dreams, too many things. We grew close as we talked.

After cleaning up dinner, I cranked opened the viewing doors. I had to use two hands to turn the crank for the dome. I turned it until the opening was facing southeast. We would be able to see Saturn. I wound up the tracking clock.

"What are we going to look at, Professor?" Rachel was standing by the ocular.

"Saturn. And I'm not a professor," I said as I walked up the wooden stairs to join her.

"How long have you been looking at stars?" she asked when I reached her.

"Since I can remember. For pay, about fifteen years.

Scoot over and I'll line up Saturn."

Rachel moved back against the railing. I stepped up to the ocular and peered in. I looked at the settings, adjusted the azimuth, then put my eye to the eyepiece again. I adjusted the knobs without looking away from the eyepiece. A moment later - voila! - Saturn. I pulled the lever to engage the tracking clock, then returned my attention back to Saturn.

Saturn's rings were tilted about fifty degrees, giving me a spectacular view. I lingered at the eyepiece as I shot the man in the car over and over.

"Stone!??"

Saturn focused in slowly. What a beautiful sight. I turned to Rachel.

"Sorry. It's just so pretty. Here," I stepped away from the ocular, "take a look."

Rachel stepped up and bent at the waist to peer in. When she sighed I knew her eye had focused.

Several minutes skimmed by as Rachel watched Saturn. My mind wouldn't release me of the guilt I felt over the men I had killed. I had to tell her. I had to make her understand that I didn't want any of it to happen. I took a deep breath.

"The first one was an accident. I was just going to net them."

Rachel turned from the telescope and looked at me. I explained about the tent, the prodding, the gunshot. I tried to explain the fear I felt when Williams said he was going to wait.

Then I told her I didn't realize the car was going so fast when I shot the tire. I confessed that the helplessness I felt when I realized the man in the back was trapped won't go away; nor the sight of him crying; nor the bullet going into his head. I let her into the depths of me, exposing my confusion and frustration over five deaths, committed by me. I lay bare the frightened child in me and cried on her shoulder, again.

This time there was no embarrassment. I wanted to open up to her. I wanted to let her in. Suddenly, in the solitude on the peak and in the observatory, I needed her. Needed her to escape from the guilt; needed her to believe in me; needed her to be genuine.

"I don't understand," I jerked out between sniffs. I was talking to her breast and listening to her heart through her chest. Rachel held me tightly to her, shhing me softly. We stayed like that for several minutes while I tried to get a hold of myself. When she spoke her voice resonated in her chest, drowning out her heartbeat.

"Let's get back to the stove. It's getting cold," she said, easing her hold on me.

I slipped out of her arms, feeling like a child of six or seven. My eyes felt puffy and my nose was running. I wiped my nose on my sleeve, then looked into her eyes. Was this woman I considered a child real? Could I believe in her? Tonight, if only for tonight, I needed her more than I've ever needed anybody.

I was scared, not afraid. There's a difference. Afraid is walking down a dark hallway at home and hearing the floor creak. Scared is knowing you didn't cause the creak. I was also disillusioned and going crazy with guilt. How could my government recruit people this way? I have always just wanted to be left alone. I never caused problems for anyone. I've always paid my taxes. And now I have five deaths on my hands because of the government and my own panic.

The bullet crashed through his skull...where am I to go now that I've gone too far..?...his blood soaking my arm.

I stepped away from Rachel and disengaged the tracking clock, then headed down the steps. "I'll go close the doors." I felt her eyes on me as I walked over to the crank handle. As the doors slowly shut, I saw Rachel out of the corner of my eye move to the stove. What did she see in me?

What did she see in me??! What was I doing?! I didn't need anybody along. I didn't need a girlfriend a decade and a half younger than me. I stopped turning the crank. Girlfriend? Was I falling in..? ...the blood splashed my face..the smell of blood and burning gasoline nauseating... I finished closing the viewing doors, then went back to the scaffolding at the ocular and blew out the candles before joining Rachel at the stove.

*   *   *

I awoke the next morning with a start, as though I had been slammed back into my body. Rachel's legs were draped over mine, her right arm on my chest. I slid from beneath her and slowly stood. I put on my shoes, grabbed my jacket, and headed for the door. I put my jacket on outside, then walked around the corner of the building to get in the sun.

We were over a mile above sea level and the morning sun painted a gold dawn. The air was crisp, clean, the sunlight warm. I removed my jacket and let the sun warm me. I stretched. The sun rose in the sky, leaving the clouds to their pristine white. I have always enjoyed the sunrise.

Rachel and I had done nothing last night. She had the only blanket laid out on the floor. I laid down on one edge and fell straight to sleep - mentally and physically exhausted. I know I dreamt, but I can't remember any of it. I thought about leaving before Rachel woke up, but realized I more than needed her around, I wanted her around; dangerous though it was.

As the air warmed and the sun slowed it's pace, I was suddenly forced to witness my memories of the last forty-eight hours.

Again, I felt the knife I held go into something that felt like a grain sack. Again I heard the moan of the dying man. Then came the shriek of the bullet as it grazed my temple. I raised my hand to my head, fingertips tenderly touching the thick scab. It was then I saw how many times I stabbed that man. Until then, I had thought I plunged the knife into his body only once. I counted seventeen lunges. I dropped my hand and the memory ended.

A crow cawed and flew on. The car getting air as it zoomed over the hill filled my vision. I turned with it and watched as it hit, then rolled endlessly into the mist. It burst into flames and I was inside the car, watching the two corpses in the front seat burn. I think I screamed when the one with me in the back asked for a favor.

"Stone?!?"

I spun around, startled. It was Rachel, yelling from the south door.

"Stone?!"

"Here!" I walked around the corner of the building.

"You okay?!"

I could hear the apprehension. I *had* screamed.

"Yeah. Be right there."

As I walked to the front door, I began to again wonder what Rachel was doing with me. I thought I understood her reason for mistrusting the government, but that didn't explain why she came with me. What did she see in someone fifteen years older? What did I see in her eyes when she looked at me? I looked up as I neared. She was waiting on the porch. What was I going to do with her?

What was I going to do with her? Phfft. What was I going to do? I've killed five men. They can't want me to fly missiles anymore. They must now just want me for murder. I stopped. Was the first one murder? It was an accident. And the second? Seventeen stab wounds? And Williams? And the car?!? I shook my head violently and started walking. Suddenly I was wanting to be held. I wanted Rachel to hold me. I nearly ran up the stairs to her.

"Why'd you scream?" The concern in her voice touched me. I reached for her hand. She met mine halfway.

"Flashback."

"This has really gotten to you."

"I've never hurt anybody in my life. And now I've killed five men." I looked down. "I feel terrible. I can't keep the memories out of my head." I squeezed her hand a little harder, then pulled her to me. "I escape in your arms. That's the only time."

Rachel squeezed back and whispered, "I love you Stone."

I jerked away, stumbling over my feet and nearly falling. "No. You can't," I blurted. "Not now."

"Why not now, Stone? Why not when you need me the most?" Rachel reached for my hand and grabbed it before I saw her move. I tried to pull away but she sunk her nails into my palm. "Answer me, Stone. I can choose who I'm going to love and when. You can't tell me not to." She shook my hand, hard. "Now why not!??"

"You don't know me. I don't know you. It can't be love."

"Love needs no reason. When you walked into the cafe yesterday morning, I fell in love with you." She shrugged. "It just happens.

"I'm coming with you Stone," she dug her nails deeper into my palm. "Do you understand?"

In her eyes I saw fear. Fear that she would lose me, not of what lay ahead. I really did want her along, but I didn't want her involved with what was going on. I dropped into her eyes and said,

"Let's go figure out what to do." I wanted to sound dejected, but I think I sounded relieved. Was I falling in love?

* * *

We were riding again. Two hours at the observatory to devise a plan and pack. I wore the helmet while Rachel wore the skull cap and goggles. I turned up the volume on the CD player and shifted up to fifth. We were running a dry river south into Mexico. In Mexico we were going to trade the bike for a car, then backtrack to my boat. It would take two days to get Mary Jane ready and I was hoping the detour to Mexico would give us those two days.

The song dropped into a drum solo and my mind wandered, haunting me with the five men I killed, the child behind me I'm falling for, and the uncertainty of my future. I concentrated on driving the motorcycle, but other thoughts still floated in. I increased speed, forcing extraneous thoughts out. The bike skidded more as I skirted obstacles. Rachel squeezed tighter.

Racing along the river bed at sixty miles per hour was dangerous for both of us, but I couldn't stand seeing those men in my head. The speed, the danger it brought, kept those thoughts out.

Forty minutes later, after passing under Interstate 15, Rachel tapped me on my stomach. She put her mouth against my helmet. She was saying something. I turned down the CD player.

"...EE!!!" came resonating through my helmet.

Rachel was off the bike before we stopped rolling, running for some bushes. I turned off the bike and set it on its side-stand, stepping across the road to urinate behind a scraggly shrub.

I was leaning on the bike, the helmet off, when Rachel returned.

"Going pretty fast, weren't we?" she challenged.

"Scared?"

Rachel looked me straight in the eyes. "Yes."

I felt bad for frightening her, but the guilt didn't compare to what I still felt for killing those men. "Sorry," I said quickly. "I had to."

"What?"

"Just trust me on the bike, okay. I know what I'm doing." I sounded more stern than I meant to and it showed in her eyes. The day was not going well. I stepped to her and put my hands on her waist. Her body felt good under my hands. I *was* falling for her.

"I'm sorry, Rachel. I didn't mean to scare you, or be so mean to you. I guess I'm scared myself."

Rachel put her arms around my neck and pulled my head down to her. Before I realized what she was doing, she kissed me. Before I realized what I was doing, I kissed her back.

...falling down a spiral, destination unknown...

I jerked away, stumbling into the motorcycle.

"Scared?" Rachel teased.

"I think so." I looked into her eyes. They had a pull. "We need to get going."

It was then I heard the helicopter. I looked up. We were in the open, stuck on the river bed. There was no where to hide. I yelled at Rachel, "Get on!"

I had the bike started and in gear when Rachel plopped down behind me. I couldn't hear the helicopter over the bike engine. It didn't matter, in the river bed it would have been difficult anyway to discern the direction. I let out the clutch and took off in the direction we had been going - south.

A moment later Rachel was screaming through the helmet, "They're behind us!!"

I switched hands on the throttle and plugged in the CD player, cranking the volume all the way up. I flipped up the visor and turned to Rachel, "HOLD ON!"

I downshifted a gear and twisted the throttle. The back tire broke free and we fishtailed until I shifted up. I could barely breathe, Rachel was holding me so tight.

The river bed veered to the right. So did we, skidding

off and on during the curve. I caught a glimpse of the helicopter from the high mirror as we turned. They were right on our tail.

We rounded the bend and came face to face with another helicopter, hovering ten feet off the deck. Instinctively I downshifted and squeezed the front brake. I caught a glimpse of a path up the left bank out of the corner of my eye. I locked up the rear wheel and skidded the back end to the right, turning us left. I downshifted, released the rear brake and gunned the throttle, shooting us towards the river bank.

We hit the path doing forty and jumped up the first ten feet. Rachel rose off the seat with me, absorbing the shocks with our knees as we climbed the thirty foot embankment. I couldn't hear the CD anymore, only my heartbeat.

We launched off the top of the path, headed for the helicopter that had been following us, now hovering a hundred yards away in front. In my peripheral vision I saw the other helicopter rising over the bank. The panic that had been building for days broke through my barriers. I screamed as we descended. We hit the ground hard and I lost control of the bike.

Chapter 6

I awoke into a throbbing headache. There was a dull ache in my right leg. Slowly I opened my eyes. I expected to see sky, but when I saw the false ceiling I remembered the helicopters. Rachel?!? I sat up and my back screamed a hot flame up the right side. I winced, then scanned the room.

The room was a small square, barely enough room to walk around the hospital bed I laid in. The walls were unpainted cinder block. There were no windows and only one door, to my right. I received a distinct impression of being under ground.

Beneath the thin sheet on the bed I was naked.

Where was Rachel? I fell back to the bed, ignoring the pain in my back and head. Did she survive the crash?

The door opened. Three men entered my cell, two in blue guard uniforms, big and burly with flat-tops, the third, a yellow tie with brown stripes peeking from beneath a white lab coat, held a clipboard. He was older than the guards, in his thirties somewhere. He had the demeanor of an attendant. The guards took their posts on either side of the door. The man in white took the extra two steps to the bed. I crossed my legs and put my hands in my lap.

"You gave us quite a scare there, Mr. Smokestone. Also quite a bit of problem." He looked up from the clipboard. "May I call you Warren?"

"No. Where's Rachel?" I couldn't believe how steady my voice was.

The man with the clipboard turned to the guards. The one on the right leaned forward and whispered something. The man in white turned back to me, his head down.

"The girl you were with, Rachel. I'm sorry. She didn't survive the accident."

I felt something in my chest grow cold. I wanted to vomit, then blamed the man in the white coat. I lunged at him, catching him at his throat. We went to floor and I heard his head crack against the linoleum covered cement. His eyes rolled up in their sockets and he went limp beneath me.

Instantly the guards were on me. I felt myself being lifted, then tossed back on the bed. My back, my leg and my head were on fire. Electric fire. I blacked out.

*   *   *

I awoke into the same headache, but the dull ache in my leg was sharp, the whole leg tingling with needles. I was also strapped down, which explained my leg. I was still naked, my groin exposed to the air.

"You awake, Smokestone?"

It was more of a demand than a question. I opened my eyes. Another man in a white coat, a black tie underneath. He didn't have a clipboard. He was older too, in his fifties. He was staring at my groin, then looked at my face.

"Ah. You are with us. I'm Doctor Hanson. Doctor Boyd will be out a few days thanks to you. With a concussion. You certainly are a violent man, Smokestone." He smiled. "But we want that, actually."

I closed my eyes, hoping I'd open them again and be home in the cabin. It had all been nothing but a dream. I opened my eyes. The pudgy Doctor Hanson was standing next to the bed. He was still standing down by my waist.

"Where am I?" I pushed out.

"You're at the Tiefort Mountains Medical Clinic. A military facility."

"What's going on? Why am I here? I'm not in the military. Why were we being chased?"

"You've suffered a mild concussion, a cracked rib and some torn ligaments in your right leg. You were lucky. You're going to be fine."

"And Rachel?"

"There was nothing we could do for her. She wasn't wearing a helmet. I'm afraid she died at the scene. I'm terribly sorry."

"Sure you are. Why were you chasing us?"

"Now now Smokestone. You're not in a position to be asking questions. I'll be.."

"Fuck you, Doc!" I wrestled with the straps, causing the fires in my body to increase intensity. "Fuck you!!"

"Inject him."

A guard stepped up and put a needle in my arm. As I slipped into the drug induced sleep, I felt a hand touch my thigh.

        *   *   *

I woke up slowly this time, groggy. It was almost as if I was hovering a short distance away, watching myself awaken, waiting for the right moment to re-enter my body. I opened my eyes, half-expecting to see myself floating above me.

The room was empty, unfocused, but empty. Then I remembered seeing Rachel recently. She was on a bus. She looked very sad. The memory was surreal, floating in ether and time.

I tried to move. I was still strapped down. I never felt so helpless. My thoughts were still slow, my eyes out of focus. I wondered what was in store for me.

Moments later an orderly came in and injected something into my IV that put me back in the surreal world of unfocused dreams.

        *   *   *

I woke up screaming into a dark world, the melting flesh dripping on my arm. The scream brought the guard, flooding the room with light from the hall. I was back, the cement cell a familiar and now sometimes welcome, sight. Something was injected then door closed. I was in the dark again.

How many days? One? Thirty? Time had no meaning here, drugged or awake. There was no day or night. No sunrise and sunset, just lights on, lights off. Drugged or getting drugged. How many days?? How many days!??

The door opened again, the orderly with the syringe entering. "Let me go," I thought I yelled. I heard, in my voice, "Llll-oooo".

The orderly looked at me, then gave me a quirk of a smile. "Hello to you," the idiot said, then sent me back into a world I was beginning to enjoy. As I felt the cement world slip away, I wondered about time in the world where I had no form.

...how many days..?

I awoke refreshed and hungry. I could move, the straps and the pains were gone. I sat up and received a head rush. I grabbed the bed until the dizziness went away. I was still naked. Suddenly I was hit with memories of being sodomised and oral sex performed on me. None of the memories had to do with Rachel. These were horrible memories. Comparable only to killing those men.

The door opened and the man in the sex memories entered. I put the pillow in my lap. There was no hate, no animosity. I just didn't want to be seen, or touched. Nor did I want anything except something to wear.

"Now now Smokestone. No need to be shy. We're friends, remember," Doctor Hanson said. He almost sounded as if he meant it. Two guards followed Hanson in and I could see two more outside.

"Where are my clothes? I want my clothes?"

Doctor Hanson turned to the guards. "Get him a gown."

"I want pants."

"A surgeon's gown." Hanson turned back to me. "How are we feeling?"

"We feel good. Thank you, Doctor Hanson."

"That's good. It's been a pleasure working with you, Smokestone," Hanson said, then smiled.

I felt wrong. Although I did feel physically well, I felt there was something wrong with the situation. Like I shouldn't be thanking them. I shouldn't be nice to these men, yet I felt I should. I should be nice and do whatever they say. After all, weren't the guards there for my protection. Didn't the doctors save my life. I was grateful, but it felt all wrong.

A guard entered carrying the gown. The guard on the left was smiling. Et tu, Brutus? I suddenly had a strong desire to brush my teeth. Hanson handed me the gown.

"You could turn around."

"Put it on," Brutus rasped.

I put the gown on, then dropped to the floor, my bare feet slapping the linoleum. The floor was cold.

"Let's go, Smokestone," Hanson said, then turned and stepped out the door. He waited in the hall, looking back at me. I didn't have much of a choice, I felt compelled to go. In bare feet I followed Hanson into the hall, the linoleum changing colour past my room door.

"Where we going?"

"You just don't learn, do you? You don't ask questions here," came a voice from behind and to the left. It was Brutus again.

"Fine. Where we going?" It was a harmless question, I thought.

Somebody from behind slapped me in the head, hard. My head slammed into my shoulder, almost knocking me unconscious. I stumbled forward and to the left, falling on Hanson. Somebody pulled me off Hanson and held me until I regained my balance.

"Easy, boys," Hanson said. "He's still fragile."

I remained silent, most of the hallway past Hanson still out of focus. I understood now: Talk when spoken to. We turned a corner and the linoleum was replaced by stone. It was rougher on my feet, but I didn't feel any pain, only the stone texture on the soles of my feet.

Just before the hallway ended, we came to a door. Hanson knocked, then opened the door. Our little group entered single file, me in the middle.

The room was bigger than my little room, but the walls were the same cinder-block. A picture of a missile leaving a silo hung behind the only desk in the large room. Two armless chairs sat facing the front of the desk, a man in a uniform with lots of brass and ribbons sat behind the desk in a leather chair. He was smoking a cigarette.

"Have a seat, Smokestone. Hanson," the man behind the desk motioned for the doctor to sit. I heard the door shut behind us.

I sat down in the chair to my left. The nameplate sitting on the desk read, "Col. V. Newton". My stomach growled.

"Hungry, Smokestone?"

I nodded.

"Sergeant!" The door opened behind me. "Get this man

some food. I'll take a donut and coffee myself. Hanson?"

Doc Hanson declined with a wave.

"That's all, Sergeant" Colonel Newton turned back to me. "Bet you have a lot of questions. Well, I'll answer them all after you've had something to eat." He turned to Hanson. "How many?"

"Ninety-five," Hanson replied.

Ninety-five what? Days? Treatments? Injections? Rapes? The colonel looked at me. "You've been here a little over five weeks Smokestone. You're ours now. From this day on you will cooperate with us fully, without question. Do you understand?"

Five weeks?!? FIVE WEEKS!?!? Then I heard myself say, very calmly, very politely, "Yes sir."

"Good," the colonel stood up and paced behind the desk, "Shortly you will begin training on a top secret project that very few have the privilege to even know about. You will be trained to operate the VCM - Video Cruise Missile. You, Warren Smokestone, will be a Remote Pilot. There are only five others. Their flying experience ranges from six months to three weeks."

My head was full of questions demanding to be answered. Again, though, I heard myself say, politely, "Yes sir."

"You will become part of this elite group of Remote Pilots. Most of them were a bit more willing than you. But it's good to see you've come around."

This wasn't right. This was all wrong. What the hell did they give me? What the hell did they do to me? Calmly, I said, "Yes sir."

There was a quick knock, then the door behind me opened and a gruff voice said, "Sir, breakfast."

"Come in, Sergeant," the colonel said, waving the man with the food inside. The Sergeant set the tray on the desk, pirouetted an about-face, and left the room without another word.

"Good soldier, that Sergeant. Now, help yourself, Smokestone."

I leaned forward and picked an apple and orange off the tray. I sat back and bit into the apple.

Chapter 7

Two days later, after being assigned a room and shown where the mess was, I was escorted to the training room.

The training room was rectangular, a small desk in the far left corner was against the wall. The rest of the cinder block room was consumed by black electronics surrounding a large, concave monitor and a sunken chair. The man behind the desk motioned for me to sit in the chair in front of the monitor. As I walked over to the chair, the last of my escorts shut the door behind him. The man behind the desk began his monologue.

"You're being trained on your governments most secret weapon, the Video Cruise Missile. Simply known as a Needle, you will learn to fly and guide your Needle to its target without flaw.

"If you will step into the simulator we can get started with your flight training. Mr. Smokestone? Would you please step into the simulator?"

Needle? VCM? Simulator? What the hell was I going to be doing? I examined the chair before climbing in. The monitor looked like a small movie theatre screen, half as wide as the room. The top edge tilted down, towards the sunken leather chair fifteen feet away.

A chrome, tubular frame hovered above the seat and screen; a small camera mounted at the rear, up high to monitor the trainee. A black curtain hung on the far side to enclose the operator.

"Mr. Smokestone. I don't want to have to call the guards back in here. Would you please sit down."

I stepped down into the V-shaped pit, the point of the V being the chair. I fell into the seat, noticing controls on either armrest. Oh, this chair is comfortable.

"On the right arm of the chair you will find a joystick. You will fly the Needle with the joystick. It does basically what you would expect a joystick to do; left for left, right for right, forward for down and back for up.

"On the left arm are three knobs. The left two control screen intensity. The knob below the headphone jack controls headphone volume. In the simulator, you don't have headphones so that knob controls speaker volume.

"Your speed is constant when you take control of the Needle. All you have to do is fly."

I could fly for hours sitting here. I played with the controls on the armrests. The joystick had a feel. Cool. This was going to be fun.

"I'm going to activate the screen now," the man behind the desk said.

I watched the monitor in front of me. It was

rectangular. It was also concave, wrapping towards me. A blue screen filled the display, data lined the bottom, the center and most prominent was the guidance bar.

"The Guidance Bar that you see at the bottom, center," I saw the line of vertical lines.

"..will move from side to side as you fly. You want to keep the course marking centered. This is the correct course. This is what you will return to after avoiding any obstacles."

Right right right. I've been in flying games before. Turn the thing on and let me fly. Come on. Come on!

"In the lower left you will see a clock. This is the Time Remaining Clock, or TRC. That is time remaining to impact. The other pilots close their eyes three seconds prior to impact. You may want to also, Mr. Smokestone. They say it helps on coming out of the Zone."

Yea yea yea. Close my eyes. Clock on left. Let's fly. Come on, let's fly!

"Also on the left is your map. Your position is indicated by the red dot. Please pay attention to sharp turns marked on the course.

"In the lower right hand corner is the gyroscope. This shows your..."

Yea yea, I know what it shows. Come on, let's fly!!

"Also there on the right is the altimeter. The numbers below it are maximum, top, and minimum, bottom."

Let's fly!!!

"During night flights and adverse weather; fog, rain, your screen will be a combination of infrared and radar images. You can switch to this image by pressing the button on the joystick handle.

"Your lessons in here will be on digitized terrain. There are no live flights in this room.

"Are you ready, Mr. Smokestone?"

I nodded my head, saliva pooling in my mouth. I swallowed. The screen came to life in a single flicker, the data on the bottom changing colours to black. The monitor showed a water scene. As driving music began to play in the background, a voice came through the speaker behind my head.

"You will fly for twelve minutes up the coast to a naval yard. There you will fly your Needle into the first ship you see. Enjoy your flight, RP."

I looked to my left, the man behind the desk had sat down. A small motor whirred and the black curtain crawled on the half-oval above me, wrapping me in darkness and the glow of the screen. The music volume increased, then the screen began to roll. A moment later, on a drum beat, I was flying.

I couldn't tell what I was flying, there was only a foot of white cone in front of me. But it did feel as though I was flying it; fast and close to the water. I adjusted the screen, then slowly, gently, moved the joystick around. I veered left a little, then right. I nosed up, then back down. I played and played, the songs repeating through the speakers and filling the room with a drum beat that kept me in the Zone.

I did a roll. Flying was different than Cycle Sin. You couldn't ride upside down in Cycle Sin. This was great. I did a barrel roll, twisting more than three times.

The speaker behind my head crackled. "Veer to the right, Smokestone. When you reach the coast, get up over land as soon as possible and follow your course marker."

Aye aye, Captain. "Yes sir." I veered right.

Moments later the coast appeared. I eased the Needle over it and was racing on the beach, hurdling rocks and skirting cliffs. The voice broke in again.

"A little further inland, Smokestone. Follow the course marker. Up and over the cliff, if you will."

I jerked the nose up and hopped on top the cliff, sliding the Needle right until I was on course. The terrain was rougher here. Over water and the beach was pretty much level flight. There was more to miss here; trees, poles, buildings, hills. I got busy. I glanced at the altimeter. I could climb another three hundred feet. That would clear me of trees and most buildings. But I stayed where I was, zipping through the terrain like a madman.

I turned up the music again, booming the bass and beat through me. I flew. I was cruisin'.

This was great. I was flying, without the G-forces. I flew over an open meadow and spun the Needle, the screen going through three hundred sixty degrees several times.

The voice crackled through the speaker again, over the music. "That's enough playing, Smokestone. You're here to fly, not play."

How am I suppose to know what this thing can do if I can't play?

"Just seeing what she can do, sir."

"You'll get plenty of that.

"Now, you're coming up to a large city. You will fly just above the highest building, staying below the ceiling on your altimeter."

"Yes sir." I looked further into the screen, anticipating the city. I hurdled a tree line, then was back on the ground, fifteen feet off the deck. The cityscape focused in a moment later and I started my climb. It wouldn't be long before I was at the city.

I did have several seconds to realize just how boring it was going to be flying over the city. I eased the nose down, entering the city through an alley, zipping over the tops of trucks.

"Smokestone," the voice was stern. I was in trouble. "Get that Needle above the city. Now, Smokestone."

"Yes sir." The course marker drifted to the left and I cut through an intersection and onto a four-lane street. The course marker came back to the center.

"Smokestone!"

I pulled the nose up at the end of the street, a T-intersection. I was almost vertical going up the side of the building. I leveled off after clearing the building and set the course marker. How boring.

I did discover why he had recommended closing my eyes before impact. It is a very abrupt way to come out of the Zone. Worse than crashing in Cycle Sin. I swear I crossed my eyes so bad that I bruised my nose.

"Nice first flight, Smokestone. You will have to abide by the rules, though. Flights through cities are strictly prohibited. We are after military targets only.

"Prepare for your second flight."

I flew for hours that first day. The average flight was six minutes. I flew seventy-two flights. They gave me five days of training before I was added to their arsenal.

Chapter 8

I had flown sixteen missions by the time I started to finally come around. Sixteen real missions. Sixteen impact missions. It was the last mission that caused something to snap inside my head. All their programming began to unravel. I began to think on my own again. I realized what I was doing, what my missions were. I wasn't a zombie anymore. I wanted out. I began looking for a way to escape.

Today was another mission, my first since *snapping*. Another truck? Another bridge? Another train? They could all be considered military targets, yes. But who's? We weren't at war with anyone. And if the other pilots have been flying longer than me, what the hell were we blowing up?

Since my first live mission, I have flown into impact with eyes wide. It is something I still cannot fathom as to the reason. Perhaps it was to break their hold on me.

The other five pilots thought there was something

wrong with me; keeping my eyes open at impact, and none of them talked to me during meal or rest periods. But that was okay, I thought there was something wrong with them for enjoying this.

    I flew a desert this mission. Rolling sand dunes and stretches of flat that left my mind room to wander. The sand provoked memories that didn't seem mine. A young woman floated to the surface, then vanished without a name. A sailboat drifted into view, then sunk into the sand. I turned up the volume to the headphones. I had to fly. Fly to impact.

    The base rushed up to me out of the horizon, an oasis. I was to make passes until I found my target - a large van housing radar equipment. I looked at the TRC. Four minutes to locate the van. Four minutes of flying through flack over the same terrain.

    I passed over the base, not seeing anybody nor recognizing any of the equipment. I pulled a loop at the end of the base and came back over the same route.

    I passed the base a second time and banked the Needle, intending on coming in from a different direction. I looked at the shadows. They would have the sun behind them this time. I dove, leveling off at headlight level.

    A man stepped out in front of me as I zoomed down the street. He aimed his gun at the Needle. I could see the muzzle blast as I raced towards him. Wasn't he going to move? I jerked the nose up, hitting the barrel of his gun and knocking him down. Whoops.

    The Needle suddenly jerked upward. It had been hit. I tried to nose it back down, but the Needle climbed relentlessly. I glanced to the TRC - two minutes remained. I removed the headphones and stepped out of the cockpit as the Needle climbed straight up.

A metallic voice entered the room. "That was not satisfactory, Smokestone. Get some sleep and we'll go again tonight."

"Yes sir."

I retraced the familiar steps to my room, my thoughts on hitting the man in the street. Visions of horrible memories flashed through my thoughts; of shooting a man in the head, of stabbing another repeatedly, of a rifle butt breaking the collar bone and rupturing a main artery. How many had I killed with the Needles? How many before flying the Needles? I had to get to sleep, though. I had a night flight coming up.

I closed the door behind me and stood there. Memories of events prior to being here began to surface. The woman I keep seeing on the flight is named Rachel. I'm an astronomer, not a Remote Pilot. I don't belong here.

"Is something wrong, Smokestone?" the metallic voice from the speaker entered the room unannounced, startling me out of my thoughts.

"I was shot down today, sir." It was my first lie. I had been shot down before, today was nothing. "I'll be fine after a nap, sir."

"Then get to sleep, Smokestone. Your flight is in six hours."

"Yes sir."

I walked over to the bed and sat down. I removed my shirt then laid back and closed my eyes. Memories came back stronger and more vivid. I had loved a long time ago. I had scanned the heavens. I had killed five men. *...how many with* *the Needle.?.* Rachel wasn't dead.

I sat up in bed. Rachel wasn't dead? How could I know this? But I did. I felt it, somehow. Then the vision of her on a bus, crying, came back.

I laid back down and tried to fall asleep. Questions and vague visions haunted me. The lights snapped on with me facing the wall, eyes wide.

"Time for you flight, Smokestone," came the disembodied voice.

"Yes sir."

"Thirty minutes to flight. There's time for breakfast. See you in the flight room."

"Yes sir."

I scooted out of bed and changed underwear. I brushed my hair back with my hands and finished dressing, then headed for the mess.

As I walked the blank corridors my mind continued its descent into the past, the young woman named Rachel returning most often. She was important. I didn't know how or why, but Rachel was important. I had to find her.

I walked into the mess hall and went straight to the serving line. I filled my tray with fresh fruit and sweet rolls before turning around to find Colonel Newton in the mess with me. We walked to a table.

"Morning, Colonel."

"Actually it's evening."

"Really." I haven't seen outside since arriving.

"They tell me you've been having nightmares."

"It's the shoot downs. I guess they're getting to me."

My second lie.

"Is that what woke you today?"

I put my tray across from the Colonel, then sat down. "Yes sir. The shoot down today was a bit bothersome."

"But it was a run out. You only lost control."

They knew about the man in the street. Duh. They knew everything here. ...*not everything*...

"In fact, you left the cockpit with two minutes to go on your TRC. You're shaken up from hitting that man with the rifle. Aren't you?"

Perfect. It would end any suspicion of me having flashbacks. "Yes sir. I..I could see his face."

"You just have to remember that they're the enemy. Man, woman or child. They're the enemy. You're just a robo..uh, Remote Pilot. Now eat."

"Yes sir." Did I show signs of catching his slip? I prayed not. I stabbed the fork into the bowl of diced fruit and thought about the screen on night flights.

"You're one of our best pilots, Smokestone. You've really come along. You are, almost single-handedly, bringing this unit out of it's infancy. If only we could get the others to fly like you. But, they're volunteers. You just can't get good hired help these days.

"You, on the other hand, had to be coaxed. You drove a hard bargain, but it was worth it. You'll like your mission tonight."

I swallowed. "Yes sir." I was going to be watched closely now.

"Good. I'll see you in the flight room." With that, Newton left the mess hall.

I finished the bowl of fruit and started in on a sweet

roll. Cameras everywhere, watching even as I sleep. I had to get out, to escape. I couldn't kill, not even by remote. But I would kill to get out.. wouldn't I? WOULDN'T I???

...yes...

Chapter 9

As I walked from the Mess Hall to the Flight Room I fought the urge to run down the corridor. I didn't even know where the exit was. How was I going to escape if I don't know where the exit is?

I looked up with my eyes, keeping my head straight. Cameras were placed every fifty feet. I knew there were microphones everywhere, too. They talk to me everywhere. Even in the restroom. How was I going to get out with so much surveillance? I felt panic begin to grow deep inside my gut. How was I going to get out?!?

I couldn't think about it any longer. I was at the Flight Room. I opened the door and stepped in, dreading the flight for the first time. As I sat down in the cockpit I wondered how I could fail the mission, respectfully.

The screen came on to the familiar blue, the data going active first. I read the TRC: 08:00. An eight minute flight. Who was I going to kill this time? That information has never been given, and I can't tell by the landscape. The map came up. A lot of sharp turns. There wouldn't be time for thinking. The altimeter came up next, followed by the gyro'. The screen would be next. I put my fingers on the joystick, closed my eyes and waited for the beep. The beep indicated you had control.

BEEP!

I opened my eyes to a dive. The Needle was headed straight down. I glanced over to the maximum flight level. It read one hundred feet. The altimeter was at five thousand. The ground rushing up to me was beautiful. Rolling, green hills flowing out flat into a plain. The plain rippled.

At a thousand feet I started to level out the Needle. At a hundred feet I was level. I dropped the Needle to twenty feet and skimmed the tall grass. I glanced down at the map. I was approaching a turn to the right. I looked as far ahead as possible. I couldn't see any landmark for the turn.

A second later a windmill popped up on the horizon. I looked to the map again. That was the landmark. Seconds later I made the hard right. Foothills were on the horizon. There was a series of turns to the left before reaching them. So far the flight had been boring, leaving me time to think.

Where would I go if I did escape? And just how am I going to escape? I've only been on this one floor and only a portion of it. All the walls were the same cinder block. Cameras and microphones were everywhere. I haven't been in a room or hallway yet that didn't have a camera.

A series of left turns came up. Time for me to get busy.

At the end of the left turns I was in a canyon. The minimum level still read twenty feet, the maximum was now two hundred. I was flying over a river that is still cutting the canyon. There wasn't time here to do anything but fly. I glanced at the TRC; less than five minutes.

Could I hit a canyon wall and get away with it? No. The walls were too far away and I had flown tighter courses without incident. No. I have to complete the mission. I can't have them suspecting anything. I have to get out and tell the world what we're doing. I have to get out and save my ass!

There it is! A dam! I glanced to the TRC; three seconds. I looked back to the screen. I could see the grain of the concrete just before the screen went white...the pistol was aimed at the top of his head, I pulled the trigger, then everything went red.

I closed my eyes. The music in the headphones slowly quieted, then died. I was back. All of me. All my memories. I watched as I drove up the river bank, Rachel behind me. I watched from above as we crested the bank and came face to face with a helicopter. I saw us go down. I saw Rachel crawling to me as men from the helicopters approached. She wasn't dead. Rachel wasn't dead! I knew it. I knew..

"Smokestone. You can exit the cockpit now."

"Yes sir." I climbed out of the seat and walked to the door. With my back to the camera, I smiled. Rachel was alive!

"Report to your room, Smokestone."

"Yes sir."

I opened the door and entered the corridor. My room was to my left. Everything was to my left. I looked to the right. The hallway stretched endlessly. I hesitated, then went to my room.

I laid down on the bed, the want of escape pushing my

mind. I couldn't remember ever seeing a weapon down here. Listen to me. Down here. I'm assuming I'm underground. I had no idea where I was or what to do. I could feel panic crawling into my gut.

If I was underground there would be plenty of opportunity to stop me. And just how far under are we? How big is the complex? Where is the complex? Tiefort Mountains sounded familiar. That is, if that was the truth.

How often do they watch the monitors for those cameras? Are the doors alarmed? And just which door is the exit? There was just too many unanswerable questions to formulate a plan. The only option that came to mind was to just start running down a corridor and play it by ear.

But that was ludicrous. I would be stopped before I reached the end of the corridor. If I had a gun..would a gun help?

I rolled over, the camera to my back, and opened my eyes. I laid awake until the voice woke me for my next meal. I hadn't come up with anything. Six hours of mental anguish and still I could only come up with running down a hall, screaming.

I went through my routine of washing and changing before heading down to the Mess Hall. Perhaps I would see another robot today. Perhaps he could tell me of an exit. Perhaps my ass. None of the other pilots talked to me.

The Mess Hall was between my room and the Flight Room. There was one T-junction on the way, and that led to the Colonel's room. You could see the end of that hallway from the Colonel's door.

I continued on to the Mess Hall where I found another robot, pilot, finishing up his meal. After I had sat down the voice came over the speaker, talking to the other pilot.

"Whitman. Your flight leaves in ten minutes."

"Yes sir," Whitman responded.

We ate in silence, sitting at opposite ends of the room. Halfway through my meal I came up with a plan. I would take a hostage.

When the other pilot left, I returned to the mess line and grabbed an apple. I also slid a fork under my shirt and into my waist band. I sat back down and ate most of the apple while I waited to be called for my flight, the fork poking into my stomach, praying to somebody's god that they had not seen me take the fork.

"Smokestone. You have no flight as of now. You will return to your room and await further orders."

"Yes sir."

I stood up with relief and nearly lost the fork down the front of my pants. The orders helped my intentions. I disposed of the trash, then left. If they saw me take the fork I would find out soon. I headed back to my room.

At the T-intersection I turned right and headed for the Colonel's room. I expected voices behind me any second as I approached his door. My heart stopped the entire minute it took to walk to his door, but there were no disembodied voices.

As I grasped the door knob, I suddenly wondered what I was going to do if he wasn't inside. I turned the knob and threw open the door.

Colonel Newton jumped in his seat, pushing the chair away from the desk.

"Smokestone! What the hell are you doing?!"

I rushed the Colonel before he could utter another

sound. On the quick trip to him, I pulled the fork from my waistband, then hurtled the desk. The next moment we were on the floor, the Colonel on his back, me on top with the fork against the Colonel's neck and my knees on his shoulders.

"You're letting me out today, Colonel." Venom dripped off every word I said.

"You know we can't let you out, Smokestone. It would be a breach of national secur-aucggh."

I pushed the fork in a little deeper, drawing blood. "I know what national security means - national dirty secrets." I twisted the fork, slightly. "And you're letting this secret go." He squirmed beneath me.

"I..can't..it's not..my aucggh."

I twisted the fork the other way. "It's your decision," I paused, "whether you die now or not." I knew I had only minutes before the guards arrived. I also knew, or at least thought I knew, that the Colonel had an emergency escape route. I was hoping it was in his office.

"Where's your escape route?"

The Colonel's eyes, startled, darted to his right, then back at me. I looked to my left. The Colonel kicked me in the butt. I fell forward, the fork plunging deep into his neck. He jerked several times before laying still.

I couldn't believe it. My hostage was dead. There was no turning back now. I had to find the escape route.

I shoved the desk against the door, then went through the drawers. I found a pistol and an extra clip, but nothing else. I rummaged through the colonel's pockets and found motorcycle keys(...the brand name was on the key and they don't make cars...). I ran to the wall and started searching for a switch. The wall was like all the rest - cinder block. The switch must be a pressure point. I ran my hands along the wall. Nothing. Wait..the remote on the key ring. Maybe it's not for a vehicle alarm.

I pulled the keys from my pocket and pushed the only button on the little gizmo. A motor whirred into life behind the wall, then a section of the wall backed away, coming apart at the seams and slid to the right. I ran through the opening, glancing back at the fork poking out of Colonel Newton's neck. I heard pounding on the door as the section of wall slid back into place. On this side were exposed hydraulic lines that worked the door rams. I shot a line, spraying red fluid on the wall and rupturing an echo through the tunnel. I turned and ran up the incline, the squatted tunnel lined with dim bulbs fifty feet apart.

The air was warm and muggy, thick. I slowed my pace after a few minutes. The tunnel was made out of poured cement, the walls smooth, arching overhead. The passage was narrow, the ceiling low. I ran a little hunched. The incline wasn't very steep, fifteen degrees at most.

Where were they? Why hadn't they come in from ahead yet? I slowed even more, listening. I stopped and held my breath, and listened.

Nothing. No one else was in the tunnel with me. Was it forgotten by all except Newton? I checked the gun, taking the safety off, then started again at a trot. How long was the tunnel? Where did it come out? My trot turned into a jogger's pace. Will they be waiting for me there? I concentrated on my pace. I would worry about what lay ahead when I got there. Right now the tunnel looked endless.

As I ran the guilt for all the people I've killed, including the Colonel, trickled into my thoughts. All the impacts with the Needle were all witnessed again. Tears started to flow, my nose began to drip. I had to stop running and get control.

I leaned over, putting my hands on my knees. My body jerked with spasms of sobs. I had to get control.

...a flash of the fork going into Newton's neck...

I had to keep going.

...the dark, green car flipping again and again and again...

I had to get out.

...Rachel...

The spasms ceased and I straightened up, wiping my nose on my sleeve. There. I was done crying like a baby. No more feeling sorry for things I have no control over. I wiped the extra tears off my cheek with my other sleeve, then wiped my nose again.

I started running, keeping unwanted thoughts out of my head by singing. I sang one of the few songs I knew.

"I've been driving all night my hands wet on the wheel, bah da dunna bah, there's a voice in my head that drives my heel, bah da dunna bah, it's my baby calling..."

I jogged, sometimes singing, sometimes just running, for what seemed hours, but it couldn't have been more than thirty minutes. The tunnel, other than being uphill, had been straight. The incline had leveled off to a few degrees sometime after I started.

Then I felt the opening; a cool, refreshing breeze brushing by me. My heart quickened. Would they be waiting?

Moments later I could see the dark silhouette of the opening. It was night.

Twenty yards from the exit I stopped. I could see the opening against the night sky; there were bars across it, no door, just bars. I drew the pistol and slowly walked to the opening, my stomach knotting up into a ball. I was scared again. What if someone was waiting? More killing? Mine, perhaps.

Ten yards from the opening I had to stop until I quit trembling. I inhaled, sucking in as much air as I could, then held it, exhaling slowly. In a few moments I had calmed myself down. I listened for sounds of humans. The only sound was the wind rustling the leaves in the trees. I inched to the opening, stopping every other step to listen.

Five yards from the opening I pushed myself against the wall, the light cutting into the tunnel was either a spotlight or the full moon. I edged along the shadowed side. I held the gun in my right hand, feeling the wall ahead with my left.

A few terrifying steps later ...*I just knew they were going to jump out and shoot me...* I touched the bars.

The metal was cold, colder than the night air. I eased my face to the bars and looked out. It was moonlight. I was facing west. The ground below me fell away at a steep angle. Tops of conifers blocked my view straight out. I was on the side of a mountain. I listened as carefully as I could. Still, I could only hear the wind. I turned my attention to the bars.

The frame was embedded into the rock. A bar door was centered in the bar frame, a key slot on the right hand side. I touched the bulge in my pocket. Maybe the key didn't go to a motorcycle. I pulled the key out of my pocket and gave it a shot. It was a key to a motorcycle.

I knelt down and looked at the lock. It was meant to keep somebody out; the screws were on the inside. The key would come in handy after all, if...

The key fit edgewise into the slot of the screw. I twisted out the first screw with ease, the rest coming with a little more trouble. I dismantled the lock and pushed on the door, the stiff hinges creaking as the door swung outward.

I waited. The wind rustled the leaves again. No other noise. No one was coming. No one was watching. Had they forgotten about the escape route? I peeked out and looked above before looking to either side. I couldn't see anyone, nor a camera. Was it to be this easy? And only the one death? *...another death...*

I stepped out of the tunnel, still wary, and looked the area over. The moonlight threw a glow that haunted the trees and gave the area an alien aura. I was out! I could not believe it. I had basically walked out of the complex. *...Newton is forked up tho'...* The escape tunnel from the Colonel's office had taken me away from the base. I was tempted to climb the mountain and take a look at the base, but there was a glow of a city to the southwest. That was my goal. I could find transportation there. I headed down the mountain side, listening for the helicopters I knew were looking for me.

As I made my way down the steep, rocky terrain, I pieced together what I thought must have happened back at the base.

It was obviously late, the wee hours, when I attacked Colonel Newton. There must have been no one watching the monitors. That gave me the time I had with Newton. And when they did finally look, it was too late. Apparently whomever was pounding on the door didn't know about the escape tunnel. I guestimated I was in the tunnel for about forty, fifty minutes. That had to be enough time to get someone to the tunnel's exit before me.

I stopped and scanned the skies. Still no helicopter. I continued my descent. Where did they think I went? There weren't any turns in the tunnel. I couldn't have come out anywhere else. Didn't they have plans of the place? Blueprints or something?

Things just didn't make sense. If they knew where I was, why didn't they come get me? If they didn't know where I was, why not?

They, whomever they are, don't want the police involved. That was evident with the chase from Sherman Peak. But I still couldn't understand the lack of searchers now.

* * *

At daybreak I was still on the mountainside and I kept an eye out for food; berries, edible plants, grubs, etc.. The desolation of the place gave me the impression I was still on military property. I pondered the question to keep going through the day, then decided in today's technology they could find me day or night. I walked as I picked and ate berries.

Shortly before noon I was down on the flat, the sun getting hotter with each foot descended. I hadn't found any water, the juice from the berries the only liquid I've had since before escaping.

I located a rock formation to crawl under an hour past

noon, away from the sun's rays and out of sight. It was about ten degrees cooler in the shade of the rock. I removed the pistol from my pants and placed it next to my head. I was asleep within minutes.

    The chill of the night air woke me. I was shivering. My clothes were wet from sweating in my sleep. Clumsily I felt around for the pistol in the dark. I found it and crawled from underneath the rock. I forced myself up, fighting the trembling that had more control than me. I had to get moving and generate some heat. Right after I could let go of the rock and stand on my own.

    I stood there several minutes shaking violently, my body trying to jumpstart itself. Again visions of the killings I committed filled my mind. Perhaps I was going to join them? Rachel flashed between those visions. Hope. Her eyes. My raison d'etre. Then a shudder and another death.

    Finally the trembling relinquished control. I caught my breath, then started out again for the glowing in the south. It was brighter tonight, closer. I rubbed my arms as I walked, trying to remember the words to any song.

    In the early morning hours of the second day, I shot a rabbit. I used a rock to open one of the shells, then to crush the contents into a fine powder. With this, some brush, and a spark off that same rock with the butt of the pistol, I had a fire and cooked it; fur and all.

    I didn't eat much of it. Most of a hind leg. The rest was a treat for the coyotes.

    I walked 'til a little past noon, then slept 'til sunset. I reached the outskirts of Barstow in the predawn hours. The streets were empty, the whir of a garbage truck a few blocks away the only noise in the otherwise quiet city. I had to find better clothes before I did anything else. Although, hunger was becoming an issue again.

I had no money, nor any way to get any. There was money in my bank account but I didn't have any ID, just a pistol. The thought of robbing a convenience store crossed my mind, but I decided it wouldn't be a good idea. If they didn't know where I was, I didn't want to let them know. I headed for some traffic lights.

I found a pair of jeans and a heavy shirt in a laundry several blocks before the traffic light. The college aged boy they belonged to was asleep on the bench in front of the washers. The dryer had stopped and the clothes were cooling. He had been asleep for a while, there was spittle drooling out of the corner of his mouth.

I needed food and transportation next. Money would be handy. I changed in an alley, then went in search of what I needed, without bringing attention to myself.

In a used car lot of about twenty-five cars I found an early model 280Z that had access out of the lot. I broke the lock for the hatchback and crawled up to the drivers seat. I located the wires to jump the car and left them dangling. When I took the car I didn't want to drive around town looking for money and food. I shut the driver's door but left it unlocked.

Down the street to my left was an intersection, to my right, the traffic light and then the laundry. I went left, stopping at the corner.

I again thought about robbing the convenient store down on the right, but that would draw attention. Behind me was a steep embankment, to the right was Highway 247 South.

Ahead was downtown Barstow. The light changed and I stood there undecided.

A man crossed the street towards me. My first thought was to run, but he wasn't wearing a suit. As he neared I took him to be another college kid. As he passed, he spoke.

"Looking to score?"

"What?" My tone was startled. I didn't expect him to say anything.

The stranger paused and turned, "Looking to score?"

I felt naive. "Score what?"

"My last bag of snort."

"Get the fuck away from me!"

"Hey! Ease off. I'm just trying to get through college, okay."

"Just, get away from me."

The dealer started walking away when something he said registered. His last bag. He should be loaded. I yelled after him.

"Hey. How much?"

The dealer turned around and stood there. I walked to him slowly. "I said, how much?"

"Thirty," he said with contempt. "Was twenty-five, but for you I'll gladly raise the price."

I reached behind me, "Let me get my wallet." When I pulled the pistol out and pointed it at him, the dealers eyes got real big.

"Okay man. You can have it for twenty-fi..uh uh, twenty."

"I want the money."

"Ah shit, man. This is for next semesters tuition. You

can't.."

"Shut up and give me the money before I just shoot you and take it anyway."

Trembling, the dealer put his hand in his back pocket. That's when I hit him with the pistol across his temple. He fell and rolled down the embankment. I ran after him, nearly tripping, hoping he too wasn't dead.

When I reached the dealer he was moaning about his leg. I looked at his legs. The right one was twisted at an unnatural angle. He screamed for a moment, then passed out when I rolled him over to get the money. Both his back pockets were stuffed with money. There must have been two hundred bills in each pocket. There was also a slick looking silver pistol tucked into his pants. I took that, too.

A quick stop at the convenient store, then on to San Diego. I scurried up the embankment, cresting the top cautiously.

*   *   *

I lowered myself into the car, placing the chili dogs and chocolate milk on the seat beside me. I eased out of the parking lot and turned towards the freeway.

When I found the entrance to the main route south a few minutes later, I pulled into a big, dirt parking lot and looked over the map I had picked up along with a full tank. It was a straight shot from here to San Diego. I had spare ID on my boat. If I could manage it I was going to sail away. I would have to find Rachel later. I turned on the radio, found a rock station, then got on the freeway. I would be in San Diego and

SmokeStone

on my boat by time the owner arrived at the car lot. I turned up the volume on the radio and started in on the chili dogs.

Chapter 10

It took almost four hours to make it to San Diego. The sun was just edging up over the horizon as I reached downtown. I was surprised to have made it. I ditched the car a mile away from the boatyard and walked the mile as the sun shortened the darkness into shrinking shadows. Forty minutes later I was standing at the fence of the boat yard, looking at where my boat should be. Mary Jane was gone!

My heart broke. Had they known about Mary Jane and took her away? They had to know about my boat. But why move it? I stood and stared at the spot where my boat used to sit. My mind went blank. Now what? Almost absently I looked around the yard. My boat was no where to be seen.

I walked away dejected, ending up on the wall next to the water, staring at the masts in the neighboring marina. What was I going to do now? I could drive to Pahrump and try to find Rachel. Then what? Sooner or later I would have to leave the country. With the government after me, I have no choice.

But I would need ID and with my boat missing I don't have anything. It was time to go underground.

I decided I would go back downtown and get a fake ID. Then off to find Rachel. Then we'll head north out of the country and...wait.

Ninety minutes and a sore ankle later - I twisted it climbing over a fence into the first marina, I found Mary Jane at the end of a dock in the third and last marina before the bay. Her masts were on, sails lashed to the boom and stay. I had never seen her in the water, nor with masts. She looked in her place, finally. I stepped easily down the dock. I could only hope it was Rachel onboard. The question as to how dismissed with a 'phfft'. It could be them, again. I didn't really care. I rebuilt her. She's mine.

There were only two other liveaboards on the dock, all the other boats were covered and tied down. My heart pounded as I approached her. I wanted desperately that it was Rachel onboard. It didn't make sense, though. I pulled the pistol from my back.

I stepped on board as easy as I could, hoping it would feel like passing wake. Holding my breath, I made my way to the cockpit and the hatch. As I laid my hand on the handle to push open the top, one of the doors swung open and hit me in my knee.

"Ouch! Fuck!"

"Stone? Is that you?"

"Rachel?" I stepped back to let her up, lowering the pistol to my side. Luckily the knee that was hit is on the same leg as the bad ankle. She climbed out into the cockpit wearing one of my T-shirts. Only the T-shirt.

"Aren't you cold?" I asked dumbfounded, the morning sun was still warming the air. I should have grabbed her and hugged her; danced and sang. But I only asked that stupid question. Her nipples were staring at me.

She looked at me as if I were a ghost. She too, was dumbfounded and only answered my stupid question. "I am now. It's warm below. Come on."

I stuffed the pistol down the back of by pants as we went below. I completely forgot about getting away as I followed Rachel down the ladder.

It was warm below deck. I could see the fire in the door window of the little copper clad wood burning stove. Rachel sat down on the bunk, pulling her feet up beside her. I sat down in the settee.

"Where have you been?" she asked. "They told me you died in the bike crash, but I knew you didn't."

"That's what they told me about you." Then I remembered where I had been and what I had done, all sexual thoughts vanished from my mind. Then I remembered about having to get away, far away. "I saw the masts are up. I take it she's ready to sail."

Rachel nodded her head.

"How's the supplies?"

"Fully stocked. I picked up groceries yesterday. Now, where have you been?"

"How?" I asked, looking around the boat.

"My Aunt Toni died."

"I'm sorry."

"Don't be. She was old and her medicine wasn't helping her anymore." Rachel looked at the fire in the stove's window. "She left the house to her long time lover, and I got most her cash, including a big chunk of the insurance money.

"Now, again, where were you?"

I stood up. "Is my stuff still up front?" Rachel nodded impatiently. I went forward and changed as I began telling her about my experience at Tiefort Mountains.

There wasn't a whole lot I could tell her about the brainwashing, only the fact that I knew I had been brainwashed when I finally came out of it. I told her what I knew about the V-Missiles and the missions. I didn't tell her about the molestation that I can't quite remember. Those memories are cloudy, and embarrassing. When I told her about Colonel Newton and the fork, she only said,

"How awful".

At the end, she asked me the obvious question.

"Why aren't they following you?"

"Far as I know, they are."

"Don't you know?"

I looked to the deck. "No. They should be though. There wasn't even a helicopter in the desert. I don't know what's going on. I first thought that They had my boat."

"Yeah, well, I didn't know where to leave a note. I hoped you would at least look around for it."

"How long were you going to wait?"

She shrugged. "I don't know? Until the money ran out."

"Okay. Now why?"

"Why what?"

"Why did you finish Mary Jane and wait?"

Rachel scooted to the edge of the bunk and leaned towards me. I could smell her breath when she spoke.

"I knew you were alive. The boat wasn't a gamble."

"You're lucky I didn't run to Mexico."

Rachel shrugged with a smile. "Destiny."

Someone stepped onto the dock a few boats down. I tensed and turned my head to listen, pistol in hand. Rachel looked at the pistol, listened to the footfalls a moment, then glanced at the clock.

"That's Chuck," she said. "He lives four boats down. He's usually up about this time." She looked to pistol. "You can put that away."

"Chuck?" I knew it was thick with jealousy, but it slipped out. I realized then, after hearing it in my own voice, how much I had come to need her. I dare not say love.

She giggled. "Yes, Chuck." She giggled some more. "He's sixty-something and has a beer belly that will keep him from ever drowning." Rachel burst out in laughter, rocking from side to side.

"What's so funny?" I must have looked pitiful, needy.

"The look on your face when I told you about Chuck. The relief. You do love me."

"Get dressed and I'll meet you on deck."

I went on deck to prepare to leave, turning on the blower to vent the engine compartment.

"So, you still don't know what branch of the government did this?" Rachel asked above the blower when she came on deck. She had on jeans and a thin sweatshirt.

"No. But I get the impression it was the Air Force. Maybe the CIA, too. Maybe not. I got out of there as soon as I came around and I didn't ask any questions before I left."

I started the little four-cylinder gasoline engine. The

engine spurted, gurgled, then fired into life. As it warmed up I walked the deck checking navigation lights, gear and lines. Before stepping next to the tiller I took in the stern mooring line, then had Rachel take in the forward line. She pushed off at the bow. I gave the engine throttle and we were off.

Were they watching? I looked back at the dock, then the shore to either side. Nothing looked out of place. If they were watching they knew how to hide.

It was too noisy to talk with the engine running, so we sat in silence and watched the water pass by. We motored until we picked up the wind just outside the marina's breakwater. I had Rachel take the tiller as I hoisted the sails. She killed the engine when the first sail was up and drawing wind.

I sat down beside Rachel at the tiller after setting the sails. I tuned them from the cockpit. In the quiet noise of a boat being pushed through the water by the wind, we discussed our next move and more.

"So, we sail to Australia and live in the Outback."

"Sounds good to me, Warren."

"How'd you find that.." I shut up when I realized that she saw my full name on the paperwork for the boat.

"Please, I prefer Stone."

"So do I. You don't look like a Warren, Stone."

"So tell me, Rachel. How did you get away?"

"I told them you kidnapped me. They let me go after a few hours of questioning. When I got back to Pahrump, I found out Aunt Toni had died the day before.

"The funeral was the next day, the reading of the will the day after. When I got all that money, I posed as your niece and put your boat in the water.

"Mary Jane's only been in the water a week. Didn't cost as much as I thought it would. I still have most of Aunt Toni's money."

"The money." I stated, then went below. I had never counted the money from the cocaine dealer. I counted out over two thousand dollars in fifties, twenties, tens and two fives. I went back on deck.

"We're good for a while," I said to Rachel.

"I came across some money in Barstow."

"How much is 'good for a while'?"

"Two grand."

Rachel whistled and rolled her eyes.

"How much do you have?" I asked bluntly.

"Just over a hundred thousand."

It was my turn to whistle. "We're good for quite a while."

"Yes."

I put my hand on the tiller, touching hers. "I'll take over now." Our eyes met. I felt all the guilt slip away. We had made it, and thanks to Aunt Toni, we were going to make it. Rachel leaned ever so slightly to me, I took up the slack and we kissed. Her lips were warm and soft. Mine against hers felt like hard scales. Our tongues met and I began thinking about the auto-tiller. It was too soon, though. We weren't far enough out.

Eight days later I was at the tiller, Rachel sitting in the cockpit on the windward side, reading a book on celestial navigation. We were hundreds of miles from any land. I looked at her, watching her read, when I saw movement on the horizon behind her.

I couldn't tell what it was, but it was leaving a thin trail of smoke close to the water behind it. From somewhere in the darkness that I call my mind came a voice with a one word scream; NEEDLE!!!

Then it all came together. They *were* watching me when I left Colonel Newton's escape tunnel. I don't know if they were watching through binoculars or satellite, but they had to have been watching, waiting. Waiting to see if I went to the press, or to find Rachel. Perhaps they lost track of Rachel, hoping I'd lead them to her, us. Then they would wait for an opportunity. Sailing away on Mary Jane gave them the perfect opportunity.

I felt like an idiot.

I reached over and untied the tender from the cleat. The tender slid away without a sound. I checked on the approaching Needle. We had less than a minute. I threw a line around the tiller, then grabbed Rachel by her arm.

"Jump! NOW!!" I screamed, then pulled her to the lee side of the boat. "Swim back the way we came," I said as I pushed her over. Then I looked over my shoulder. I could see the fins of the Needle. I followed her a half-second later. Underwater I felt, then heard the explosion.

...eight days. I got to sail her eight days...

The shock wave kept me under longer than I wanted and I surfaced coughing out water. Rachel was calling for me, terror in her voice. She was facing away from me, treading water. I swam for her.

When I reached her she nearly jumped out of the water and ran across the surface. She spun around quick enough to cause an eddy. "I...I..," she sniffed, then coughed. "I thought you didn't make it."

    I said nothing. I pulled her close and kissed her.

    "What happened?" she asked after the kiss.

    I looked to the remains of Mary Jane. "It was a Needle." I looked to Rachel. "A Needle." I looked back to Mary Jane. "They think we're dead now. There should be no more surprises." I thought of the other pilots still back at Tiefort Mountain. How they would close their eyes some seconds before impact. I counted five before being hit with the shock wave. I wondered for months if he saw us go over the side.

    "Come on. The tender's over this way."

    Two days later a Belgium freighter nearly ran us over, then hauled us aboard. It was bound for Sydney.

    Rachel and I got married in Sydney, then bought a few acres of land *somewhere*, and have been living there ever since.

    I hesitate to say happily ever after because of what we, I, went through. We have sex maybe once a month. It's my fault. Nearly every time she touches me, I can't help but feel it's the men back at Ticfort Mountain with their hands on me; though I still don't have any clear memories of them doing anything.

    Rachel is understanding, most of the time. We have had some memorable fights, though. That, again, is me. My mood swings can occur on an hourly basis. Rachel has even accused me of having PMS.

    We don't have a television, a computer, anything with a screen. The only thing we have electronic is a stereo and the microwave, and I refuse to use the microwave.

    I don't have a motorcycle. We don't have an

automobile. We have an ancient pick-up truck, for emergencies and the bi-annual re-supply. Mostly, we ride horses. Nearly every day. Usually it's to take care of something on the property, but I enjoy it every time.

    I have the occasional nightmare now and again. I wake up screaming, often drenched in sweat and trembling. Before Rachel lights the lamp I see those men I killed, walking through a blank mist towards me.

Pillow Fight

Again, it is night. There are no sounds in my lonely room, save for the voices inside my head. And the night seems to make them worse, for the voices are loudest when it is dark.

They, the voices inside my head, scream obscenities at me. They scream of suicide. They haunt me with murders I've never committed. They unleash the beast and he roams the dungeon halls.

And too, they whisper, these voices inside my head. On their hushed breath come rumors of love, promises of warm caresses. They whisper of a tranquil cove and tropical breezes They describe the serenity of holding her in my arms.

The voices inside my head, they kiss and soothe, they cut and pierce. They tell me of a man who's face is sliding off his head, his chemically eaten arm clutching my tattered shirt as I try to escape. I can smell his breath of rotten flesh as he tells me I'm next to die.

Pillow Fight

"I'm gonna kill you," he's screaming at me over and over again. A gargling, bubbling scream as blood and spit drips from the corners of his mouth.

I try to back away from him, pounding on his arm that has a grip on me. I strike it repeatedly with my rifle butt. Still he creeps towards me, the distance between us neither decreasing nor expanding. I'm terrified. My legs stiffen and weigh like lead. I want to hit him in the head, but the sight envisioned by my mind as his head explodes beneath the rifle butt stifles me.

I think if I can just hold him off, he'll die soon. His face is nearly gone now. I can see bone and his eyes are about ready to fall out of their sockets, yet there's a spark in his bobbing eyes. A spark of hatred, revenge, or perhaps just evil.

My body burns where his arm has dripped. I force my legs to move faster, my arm to swing harder - and suddenly I'm free; of his grip, of his horrid breath, of his melting face and his unnerving threats. And I'm falling...

...falling through thick clouds. Clouds so thick they slow my fall. Soon, my descent is slower than a feather. The clouds smell good, moist, easy to inhale. Colors swirl through the clouds as they float by me, each one an individual. The clouds temp me with splendid walks along their crests, fast sails through their billows and effortless flight beside them. I ask about the man with the melting face and the clouds grow cold. My descent stops. I hover and the colors stream by me, leaving. Shivering, I try to move, finding it easier to shiver. I'm tired, very tired and I can't feel anything...

...anything but her soft hand on my cheek, her

transparent eyes piercing my soul. It had only been hours, but I had known her for years. And she, the woman with the clear, green eyes, turns the pages of my soul. I feel my heart beat when she enters the room, pain draining from my body. Then she'll touch my hand and look into me. Again, I'm falling...

...falling, hitting the floor hard, the rifle sliding from me. Then he's on me, the man with the melting face. His face inches from mine, the flesh dripping into my screaming mouth. I gag and choke...

...then jolt awake, coughing. The room is dark, the sheets wet with sweat. I check the clock - 3:03. Confused, I turn on a small light. Deciding I've slept enough, I rise and begin packing.

But lately, as I've been preparing for the killing, my mind has been, uh, bothering me. Probably where the nightmares come from.

I put the rifles in the duffel bag, then start in on the clips. As I load the clips my mind drifts, then the whine starts, inside my head, building. Building! I push another round into a clip and wonder where it will end it's quick journey. What life will this one end? I briefly survey the small arsenal in front of me - all the blood, violence, all the killing, washing over my eyes as I stare at my weapons, a cold, hollowness in my face.

This is my job, or so they tell me; to kill those who would end our way of life. I ask myself, if ours is so good, why are our enemies trying to put a stop to it? And after what we have done in the name of profit and progress, I wonder if our way is worth fighting for?

Without warning my mind takes me on a journey of it's own: I see the bullet between my fingers entering flesh, an

Pillow Fight

explosion of blood and bone. I feel the wet heat splash on me. The body drops to the floor, lifeless. I choke. My mind continues. Another bullet. This one to the skull. Part of the brain is splattered on a comrade, then he, too, is struck by one of my metal comrades. His flesh is ripped from his arm as the bullet travels it to the chest. Blood gushes from his mouth and the gaping wound.

I drop the clip and stare blankly at the wooden floor where the clip came to rest. I can ready myself for battle nearly mindlessly. Plan meticulously. Carry out the plan; crawling through ditches and sewer pipes, hiding in places no one would imagine a human would go, kill those intended, and sleep without nightmares - until now.

I had been wondering, however, that, if because of the lack of nightmares, have I become one of them? Does killing for my country ease my conscience? Does it make it right? Where is the glory now?

But now..now it is kill or be killed, survival of the fittest, shrewdest, cruelest. And I can kill so effectively, so efficiently, so coldly. I was told early in the war that I was a natural. Is this my purpose..to kill my fellow man? Is this what God has planned for me?

God? What god would allow us to do what we've done? What god would create the universe just for us? Then, from the dark recesses of my mind, where I seldom visit, a simple, fluid voice whispers;

"He who lives by the sword, shall die by the sword."

So, do I stand tomorrow? In the heat of battle, do I simply stand up and into the open? End the killing.

The hour grows late. I put the last weapon in the bag

and look to the stars. Soon, very soon, the sun will rise again on this place ravaged by man. I'm ashamed to be to be a part of it.

    My head hurts. I'm tired. And somehow I know, the nightmares will continue.

Pipe Dreams

The Pipe

  Crouched low on the screaming cycle, I race through the four meter concrete tunnel. Amber lights, at eye level on either side of the pipe, a blurry line of poor illumination. The light from the cycle's three headlights fill the dim tunnel several meters short of my stopping distance. The walls are steel reinforced. They are seamless. The little lights in the side of the walls are the only bumps you feel. Tinted goggles protect my eyes from the wind, skill from painting the walls.

  I ride for the Crucial Cycle Express; CCE. I am a Rider. I'm zoned, in a trance, conscious thought absent, the mind released from emotion and reason to react - *instantly*. Hugged tightly between my knees is a low, powerful and tough, two-wheeled machine. It has a top speed of 400 kilometers an hour, a cruising speed a comfortable 320 km/h. I was cruising, comfortably, at three-fifty.

Eight hours ago I started this run, leaving the Ancient City of Atlanta en route to the Ancient City of Tucson on the coast, via the westbound tunnel.

The tunnels, built during the Apocalypse and completed just before the Nascence, were originally for bullet shaped shuttles that were to zoom through the tunnel at twice or more our top speed. They had one shuttle run, east to west. It ended just west of the Ancient City of Tucson when the World shifted. That tunnel, which led to a place called Elay, fell to the ground. The shuttle launched through the opening and burst into flames on impact. There is nothing past the Ancient City of Tucson now but water.

Although it wasn't in my headlights yet, I was approaching an S-curve that was going to put me through a loop around the tunnel. I made sure of my seat position then squeezed tighter on the pads on the fuel tank before increasing throttle.

I love this part.

The tunnel bent to the right and I was suddenly on the left wall, riding over the skid marks left long ago by early Riders. Up to the lights, the little bumps from their frames coming through the handle bars in a rapid rhythm. The curve sharpened, sending me further up the side and off the lights. Then it eased, straightening out, sliding me back down towards the bottom.

Milliseconds ahead I saw the tunnel turn back the other way and I gave the cycle some more throttle. As my speed slightly increased I leaned to the left, zipping across the bottom of the tunnel as I reached the turn.

Up the right side of the tunnel I went, quickly riding through the top and down the other side, across the bottom and up the right side again, settling just below the lights as the tunnel curved back left. My head spun as my equilibrium returned.

Moments later I crossed the bottom again, rocking off the left wall before settling on the bottom, going straight. I eased back the throttle, settling to cruising speed. The next maneuver was fifty kilometers away, about ten minutes. Not enough time for a nap. I thought about the maneuver coming up.

Seven minutes ahead the tunnel turns downhill, rather quickly, descending steeply for eight kilometers - about ninety seconds of heart-stopping terror.

I love it.

Two minutes away I will start rocking up and down either side of the tunnel. That gives me enough momentum to shoot up either side as the pipe turns down, hitting the top just as the tunnel slopes down, riding upside-down for four or five seconds before sliding down to the bottom.

I really do love it.

I think briefly of Alina. Wondering why I miss her so when it is in my nature to be alone. I can get to missing that girl - very unlike me. Then all too quickly, it is time for me to start the pendulum.

I go up the left side first, an unexplained preference of mine, and give the cycle throttle. I can almost make the amber lights before I have to end my ascent. I lean against the fall and zip across the bottom, clicking over the lights on the other side before having to descend. Three more swings of the pendulum and I can see the bend ahead, the tire marks on the top. But, where are the weave marks on the sides? The tire marks that guides our swing?

My heart pounds, my breath vibrating with the beat. Thirty seconds to the flip and the weave marks on both sides of the tunnel have been cleaned off! My heart stops. It was either try to slow down and crawl over the round-down, or trust my ability. I tried to swallow, continuing to weave.

Twenty seconds. I continue to pendulum back and forth across the bottom of the tunnel, getting higher up the side with each swing. It looked right. I can do this. Fifteen seconds. Hardly notice the marks anymore, anyway. It felt right. Too late to slow down now. More throttle. I was going for it, sweat running down my back, my heart pounding a body shaking pulse.

Realizing that I had been relying on the tire marks too much, I inhale through my nostrils, hold it a moment, then exhale sharply out slightly, puckered lips.

Five seconds. I was going up as high as I could on either side without rolling across the top. I felt nothing but the weight and vibrations of the cycle and the effects of the forces involved. While somewhere inside a voice is screaming as loud as it can that I'm going to paint the walls, I increase throttle as I head down the left side. Two seconds. One...

Up the right side I pushed the cycle, forcing it to the top of the tunnel just as the tunnel turned down. Perfect, almost. I was pushed deeper into the seat than usual, the shocks compressing severely. Going too fast. This was going to be a rough one.

Pipe Dreams

As the cycle recoiled from the compression, it tried to come off the ceiling. I downshifted with just a pinch of clutch and twisted full throttle, leaning to the handlebars until I was kissing the gauges. I tilted the cycle and quickly slid down the left side of the tunnel to the bottom, my clothes under the windsuit wet with sweat.

I applied the brake to give me a few seconds to recover, raising to ram force air into my lungs. The air was stale, musty, and dry.

That was close. That one I didn't love. That's what I get for losing concentration. The maneuver at the bottom when the tunnel leveled out didn't require a roll across the top, but it was possible and I felt I needed it: A boost to my esteem. My heart began to pound again when I let off the brake, the speed increasing naturally.

I have been riding these pipes since I was fourteen. I know what I'm doing. This was a first for me. I have never messed up that bad before. I lost all the mail and documents, once, having to walk back through the tunnel for a kilometer collecting every piece; ran out of fuel more than once; been going the wrong way at the wrong time, once, before the second tunnel was built. Scared us both so bad we stopped and talked about it right there in the tunnel.

Those all happened years ago, though. When I was still a rookie. But the guide marks being cleaned off the sides of the tunnel caused my concentration to slip for a moment. And that is all it takes at three hundred kilometers an hour. I had almost painted the sides back there.

Why would they clean off the guide marks? Everybody knows we use them. The group in charge of the tunnel wouldn't put us at risk.. Would they? I wondered if they cleaned both tunnels.

The bottom was getting close. The guide marks were missing, but it was no surprise this time. Still, I needed to concentrate. I pushed my mind clear and squeezed the fuel tank.

I do love this part.

I was on the right wall just before the joint, aiming for the left side through the bend. I held my breath as I crossed through the top, hearing my blood surge through the capillaries in my ears, my chest ripping at the seams. Up and around, twice, thrice. My vision blurred, then fell in on itself before returning to normal while a couple of short pendulum swings settle me at the bottom.

Whoa.

Yeah, I do love it. Whoa!

The route was straight for about an hour now. I needed a nap. I slowed the cycle to around two-eighty and locked the throttle. Then, slipping my elbows through the cables, I propped myself on the handlebars.

I was tired, thirsty, hungry, and achy. Maybe I was getting too old for this. I am twenty-nine. I put my head on my arms and closed my eyes.

I swayed a only little before I was lightly asleep, deep enough to lose the discomforts of the body but not all sensation: A tilt of the cycle only a one degree was going to wake me up.

My mind, however, tortured me at times like this, unanswerable questions floating in and out of thought.

Why did the radio waves drive our ancestors mad? Is

the ice going to keep receding? Will Alina say yes, or break my heart? Why do I crave her so? Would she ever leave me?

I jerked up, the cycle wobbling as I reached for the grips. It was silly, I knew. Alina loved me. Still, I had to get to RS-6. Suddenly I needed to hold Alina. I pushed the tachometer into the red.

Alina is twenty-two, a Star Gazer. What she sees in me I have no idea. But I hope she always sees it. She is the only child of Seth, operator of RS-6.

Seth has been a friend of mine for nearly twenty years. I met him before I started riding, Alina was seven then.

When Alina and I started noticing each other, he helped our little romance from behind the scenes. Neither Alina nor I knew what the old man was doing until after we had fallen in love. That was two years ago and we have forgiven Seth for his interference.

I looked at the water and temperature gauges, both a bit warm but still acceptable. I continued at my current speed, Alina's powder blue eyes on the other side of my goggles.

I feel guilty about her sometimes. Guilty that I don't do more for her, hold her more, tell her that I love her more. I fear the intimacy, though. Unreasonable, given her beauty. Down right silly, looking into those eyes.

Perhaps she *should* find somebody else?

I closed my eyes and shook my head, forcing the thought out of my mind. I am allowed to love. Rider or not. Clear hair or not. Webbing or not.

I pushed the needle into the red a little bit further, fantasizing about finding Alina alone at the observatory.

The Cycles

Motorcycles, five hundred and three of them, were found in crates in the ruins of the Ancient City of Tucson a hundred and eight years ago. Along with the crates were boxes of parts and tools and books on how to put it all together. There were also boxes of trinkets and gadgets that don't fit any of the motorcycles, plus flimsy books with a lot pictures of life before the Apocalypse. It was all buried under a ground level floor with six meters of rubble on top. Our archeologists and other scientific minds do not understand how everything lasted so well for so long.

Me and about twenty others don't care. We are glad they did. We are also glad they figured out how to make fuel for the things out of an oil from seeds.

RS-6

RS-6 is the sixth Run-Stop running west, RS-1 the first one out of the Ancient City of Atlanta on the east coast. RS-7 is just east of the Ancient City of Tucson on the west coast.

Run-Stops are roughly four hundred kilometers apart, about two hours, the cycles needing refueling at each one. RS-6 is the smallest of the Run-Stops with nine domes, including the four used by the operator. RS-5 has eleven domes, the others have between fifteen and twenty-one domes. 'Six is also the only Run-Stop without an enclosed garden.

The domes of the Run-Stops, and most villages, are

made out of the surrounding soil. The entire structure is fired from the inside; cooking the soil mix into brick-rock. Tapestry panels the inside. The largest domes are about seven meters in diameter, the majority built having a diameter of four to six. Arched passageways three meters high connect the domes.

The nine domes at RS-6 are: the CCE Dome, Area Central, Seth's quarters(3 domes); the Food dome, the Science and two Berthing domes. Scattered about the grounds were four individual domes of merchants.

I coasted through the opening on the right of the tunnel and onto the empty platform. I pulled the cycle onto its center stand in the far corner. The platform was just big enough for two cycles on the platform. I grabbed the CCE bags and went out the door.

As I climbed down the ladder to the archway, I looked up through the skylight. Framed in dark, oily wood was the bright, blue sky of a sunny, spring afternoon. It was about midday, sunlight still striking the floor.

The house of my late parents is in a small village of thirty people, between RS-5 and RS-6, closer to 'Six. As a boy I use to walk the hour across the desert to 'Six and watch the Riders leave as I stood breathless on the platform, gaining my desire to ride as my imagination followed them down the pipe. Some of them would feed my desire with tales of riding the ceiling, the top of the tunnel, for seconds at a time.

Now, I run the tunnels, riding the top for seconds at a time. And now it is I who fill the young boys minds with stories of defying gravity. Today, there is no one.

I stepped off the ladder and walked the hundred meters through the archway alone, windows and skylights illuminating the barren, straight corridor. At the end of the archway was the CCE Dome. Everything that went through the tunnel passed through that dome.

The crowd inside the dome was small, three people. I knew two of them, nodding as I put the bags on the counter.

"Hey, this is unexpected. How you doing, Ben?" Joshua greeted me with a quick glance. "Hope you're bringing good news." He twisted the bags around, opened the top one and reached in, pulling out a small, neat stack of papers. He started reading.

"The cycle needs fuel and a looking over."

Joshua looked up, "A looking over? Why?"

"I hit the top kinda hard on the drop this side of 'Five."

"That doesn't sound like you."

I shrugged. "Who cleaned off the weave marks?" I was a bit embarrassed, I shouldn't have lost concentration.

"I told them it was a bad idea. Seth told them, too." Joshua looked back to the papers.

"TM did that?!" I couldn't believe it. Tunnel Maintenance was suppose to keep the pipe in optimum *running* condition. Cleaning off our guide marks isn't optimum for us.

Joshua nodded.

"Who's idea was that?" I hoped I sounded calm, curious.

Joshua sighed and put the papers down. "Quentin's. There were no scheduled runs for a few days and so he had the tire marks cleaned off."

"Did he ask a Rider about the idea?"

Joshua shook his head. "You know he thinks he knows it all. He thinks you guys are crazy from them engine waves, too."

"Yet he wants to spruce up the tunnels for us." I put my elbows on the counter and leaned towards Joshua. "I think all the Nobles are crazy."

"I think you're crazy. Speeding down them pipes, flipping around inside like a loose ball. I think they might be right about them spark plugs." Joshua raised his brow and nodded his head once, "Them radio waves."

I held back a smile. The frequency emitted by the ignition system is harmless. The radio waves that caused the great madness came from the towers and satellites that peppered the land and dotted the sky. But this argument has been going on since the first cycle was started seventy-five years ago. I simply shrugged. "Seen Seth?"

His attention turned to the papers, Joshua pointed right without looking up. "Area Central. Where else?"

"Thanks."

"Here," Joshua halted, "take this with you." He held out a file marked for 'Seth's Eyes Only'.

I unzipped my windsuit part way as I went through the archway leading to Area Central, the damp underclothes underneath chilling my skin at the opening. I pulled the zipper halfway back up.

Nobles. Hmph. Direct descendants of the survivors. Hmph! We all are, biologically, direct descendants, brothers and sisters.

Seth was behind his desk when I entered the dome. He looked up when he heard the door shut, his smile indicating I was a pleasant surprise. He removed his reading glasses and stood as I approached.

Pipe Dreams

Reading glasses?

"Ben!" Seth's excitement was genuine. "Good to see you, my boy."

It had been too long since I was here for more than fuel and bags. This time wasn't going to be much different, though.

Seth is shorter than me by a head. I handed the file to him. He threw the file on his desk and reached out to me. I hugged him, my arms passing over his shoulders. I pulled him close. "Finally got your glasses," I said.

Smaller than me, Seth was still strong. Even at his age he forced me to exhale as he squeezed me waist high, lifting me ten or fifteen centimeters off the floor. He put me down and backed away, grabbing his glasses and putting them on after returning to face me.

"Now I can see what your eyes say."

Seth looked regal in his new glasses, his powder blue eyes slightly enlarged. The wire rims somehow indicated intelligence. Impressions. I smiled at him, holding back a giggle. "You look good, Seth. Now it looks like you should be running this place."

"It's another milestone for our generation, Ben. Eyeglasses," Seth promoted, ignoring my smart ass remark. He has been ignoring them for years. "It's a cruel joke of Nature. Taking away your eyesight when reading is about all there is left to do for an old man." Then Seth smiled, grinning like a boy with a frog in his pocket. "Personally, I think it's superb.

"Something I've missed for the last year. Missed terribly." He sounded sadder than he should have. He turned away before I could see his face, head down.

"Now," Seth said, looking over the top of his glasses as

he made his way back behind the desk, "what brings you here?"

"I was missing you and Alina. And when the call came for a volunteer to make this run, I put my hand up."

"That must have shocked Roger."

"He made me swear I wouldn't peek."

Seth looked at me over his glasses, "Did you?"

"No." I hadn't. This was one of the few times I *hadn't* opened the bags I was carrying, I wanted to get here, to Alina. "That was a long time ago, *and* an accident."

"And you've never opened a bag since, have you?" Seth peeked over his glasses.

I stared at his eyebrows, "No." I lied. Seth knew I was lying, but that did not make it anymore right. I never read the personal letters, honest. Only the official documents. "Where's Alina?"

"Looking at solar flares," Seth lied. I could hear it in his voice. He removed his glasses and looked at me, grabbing my eyes. "She misses you, Rider."

Rider. My choice of activity isn't really conducive for marriage. I, like the other Riders, don't have a home. We are on the go too much to warrant a dome of our own. All the Run-Stops have some place for us to eat and sleep. Rarely do we stay anywhere more than two weeks. Hmph, rarely for longer than four days.

There is also a relatively high mortality rate among Riders; two or three riders killed each year. All above forty in age. And if you don't paint yourself on the side of the tunnel, having your body beat up for years leaves some with debilitating back problems. And, then there are the rumors of the 'Radio-Wave Madness'.

"You know I love her, Seth. It's just been really busy the past six months." Seth knew what I was talking about, he read the documents, too. The recent excavations of more ancient cities was bringing new information almost daily that needed to be distributed, dissected, digested, and determined usable or not. I have found it interesting, and troubling, what the Nobles decide is usable to the rest of us. "I only have a few hours before I need to be back in the pipe as it is."

"That's a shame. Will you have enough time to see her?"

"I'll make the time."

"I know how much you love her, Ben. That's why I wish you would hurry up and marry her." Seth dropped his eyes, a smile creeping into his features. "You going to ask her this time through?"

I have been planning on leaving CCE when I turn thirty in eight months, a plan started shortly after noticing Alina. Seth and I have discussed my leaving. He has a position for me when I do. What we have not discussed is that I have been planning to ask her to be my mate for three months now. Maybe it would be this time through. I almost told Seth this, but decided to wait until after seeing Alina. He'll be the third to know.

"I'm going to grab something to eat on the way out to her."

Seth's expression changed, his eyes holding a sadness, a terrible sadness. There was something wrong. Quite possibly terribly wrong. But she misses me. That was good news. Suddenly I wasn't hungry.

"What's it like outside?" The hour walk to the observatory was all outside, across the desert to the edge of the plateau.

"Sunny and warm. Take a horse."

Only twenty minutes to the observatory. "Thanks."

As I walked across the yard to the berthing dome, I found myself troubled by Seth's manner. Now, as it replays, I notice the difference in Seth. It had to be a terrible thing coming. His sadness was for a great number.

At the berthing dome I stopped by my locker and removed my windsuit, putting on pants and shirt. I changed my shoes, then headed for the stable.

I met no one on the upgrade to the observatory, which isn't surprising. There's only five hundred people in the surrounding two thousand square kilometers that 'Six monitors, and most of them are south and east of 'Six. I liked the solitude. My thoughts revolved around being with Alina.

What was she going to tell me that made Seth's eyes so sad? Will her eyes hold the same sadness that her father's try to hide?

I reached the observatory and let the mare wander, she knew the water trough was located on the north side. My shirt was wet under the arms and down the sides and back. My hair stuck to my forehead, sweat still sliding down my cheeks. I was hot, too. The mare and I had made the ride in fifteen minutes.

The observatory was a tall, adobe brick building, taller than it was round. The top opened completely to expose the telescope. I shaded my eyes with my hand and looked at the top. It was unoccupied.

I pushed open the door and walked into the cool, dim

room. A fibre board scaffolding blocked most of the sun's rays. There were no inner walls, only columns holding up the floor above and a ladder in the center of the room leading to the scaffolding. A single desk was near the ladder, a small table with an oil lamp to my left. Along the wall to my right were shelves of books reaching back to the table on my left. The bookshelf was interrupted by a single door off to my right. I closed my eyes so they would adjust quicker, still expecting to hear Alina call out to me from above. Instead, I heard the other door open, the light from outside glowing through my eyelids. She had been at the cliff's edge.

"Benjamin!"

Alina. My heart flipped. I waited until the door was shut before opening my eyes. She was walking towards me. "I saw somebody coming this way but couldn't tell who it was. I'm sure glad it was you." She slid her arms around my waist, laying her head on my chest.

I held her tight. Her long, colorless, transparent hair was warm from the sun. I inhaled the aroma and saw a meadow. All my aches slid from consciousness. "I love you," I whispered in her ear.

Alina jerked. She was crying. I knew I didn't say those three little words that often, but not that infrequent. Something was wrong. I pulled away. "Tell me."

She looked at me, the blue of her eyes besieged by glassy pink. She had been crying for a while. I could see the puffiness.

"We're all going to die," she sniffed.

I blinked. She was serious. "What?! How?" Possibilities flashed through my mind. "Is the ice coming back?" Alina shook her head. "Is..." I had almost told her what I saw in those first papers so many years ago in the tunnel.

She looked up at me and sniffed. "What?"

I shrugged. "I dunno. What else could happen?" I wiped a tear from her cheek.

"An asteroid," she resigned.

I was stunned. Our ancestors had once feared being destroyed by a celestial visitor. Instead, the insanity caused by their exposure to radio waves drove them to blow the planet up with nuclear weapons. She was wrong, in error, mistaken. "There's a mistake?" I hoped.

Alina gently took my hand, "Let's go outside."

We didn't speak as we walked to the edge of the plateau. I thought about those first papers I read after becoming a Rider. They talked about an archeological find of nuclear missiles buried in the ground, in supposed working order. Remnants of a by-gone lunacy. They almost wiped out every living thing when they went off.

We sat dangerously close to the edge, our feet resting on rocks over the side. The drop was almost straight, a kilometer to the bottom. We looked out over the flat terrain below to the water on the horizon. The tunnel was off to our left, dropping just past the cliff's edge.

Our ancestors had survived the radiation and blackness, then the persistent cold and advancing glaciers through generations. Now, as the ice recedes and summers get longer, a rock from space was coming to finish us off. Why didn't I ask Alina to marry me three months ago? Two years ago?

"How long do we have?" I asked the horizon.

She took my hand. Our eyes met. "I found it last night. I figure forty hours. Maybe less."

I turned away. Silence. Forty hours.

She squeezed my hand.

I squeezed back as I asked, "Where is it going to hit?"

"I..I can't tell. It's still too far away." She turned back to the expanse before us. "By my calculations it won't matter." She turned back to my eyes. "It's big, Benjamin. Huge."

I tried again, "And there's no chance it won't hit us at all?"

Alina shook her head, "Not really." She looked away, past her feet. "It's too close to tell."

There were other observatories. Two near the Ancient City of Atlanta alone. "Has anyone else seen it?"

"I imagine that's what you brought. Confirmation." She looked up to me, her eyes diving into mine. "I'm glad it was you."

I leaned towards her, pulled by her eyes. "Me, too."

She tilted my way and we touched lips. I pulled away, nervous, my heart racing. I was caught in a whirlpool of emotion; wanting to run as far away as I could from the rock falling from space; wanting to push Alina to the ground and make love to her until the asteroid hits; wanting to get back in the tunnel and ride. Then suddenly, without prior warning, I spoke;

"Marry me?"

Her questioning, sad eyes suddenly brightened. "Of course. Now?"

I dropped my gaze to the form in her blouse made by her small breasts. My mind, however, was in the tunnel.

"Nnno. I have to get back in the pipe. Finish delivering the good news." I wanted to stay, marry her, be with her until the end, but I also wanted to go, still scared to be with her at all.

"It won't take long. Dad can marry us," she proposed.

"No. I would still have to leave afterwards. Let me finish the run to the west coast. I'll be back in a few hours. We'll do it then."

"I don't want you to go at all."

"Neither do I," I lied. Shame on me. Twice in one day. And to people I love. "I have to, everyone deserves to know. And, maybe there's something we can do." The missiles were scratching at the corner of my mind. But I wasn't even sure they existed, let alone worked. Quentin would know. Suddenly the tire marks in the tunnel weren't very important at all.

It was four hours to the coast and I needed sleep. I also needed to get going. Time was suddenly very important. It was running out.

"Please stay."

It was almost a plea as I moved to stand.

"Let's enjoy the little time we have left together. You've given enough of your life to them. And it's going to be gone soon." She looked out over the land below. "All our efforts for nothing."

I offered my hand and I pulled her to her feet and into my arms. I held her tightly, fighting the urge to push her away and run screaming over the cliff. She did feel good, though. Her narrow frame fit snugly inside my arms. "There were survivors for the Nascence." I kissed the top of her head. "Maybe we'll be the ones to survive this time. I gotta go."

She looked up to me, her eyes sadder than then just

moments ago. "I don't know if I want to survive what's coming."

On the walk back to the observatory, I told Alina about the missiles. She seemed unimpressed.

"Don't you think we could use them to stop the asteroid?" I asked.

"I doubt it. It's pretty big."

"There's got to be something we can do?"

She thought a moment. "How many are there?"

I shrugged. "I don't remember seeing any numbers. But I know who would know. He would also know if they work."

"Who?"

I cocked my head at her, pushing my lips to the high side.

"Quentin," she surmised.

I nodded.

I rode back to RS-6 by myself. Alina said she wanted to check calculations. Maybe there was a chance.

I found Seth in the berthing dome, waiting for me.

"Did you ask her before or after she told you?"

"After." I stepped over to my locker and opened it. "The file?"

"Confirmation." He sounded like I felt, exhausted. "They give us forty-eight hours, four hours ago." He watched as I removed the windsuit and riding boots from the locker.

"Going to spread the word?"

"I have to," I said without looking at him. I wiggled into the windsuit, a long-sleeved leather jumpsuit that fit rather snug when all the zippers at the extremities were zipped.

I sat down on the bench to put on the black, calf-high

riding boots. "Did I ever tell you what I read that first time?" The boot slapped the sole of my foot. I reached for the other boot.

"No, you didn't."

I pushed my foot into the other boot, then stood, turning to face him. "It said there were nuclear missiles on the east coast and that they worked."

All the color drained from Seth's face. I thought he was going to faint. "No," he said to the floor. "It can't be true. They were all used a thousand years ago." He looked up at me. "Even if some did survive, they'd be useless. Rusty relics."

"I don't know, Seth. I do remember there were a lot of pages about them. Too many for them to be useless." Then it dawned on me, Seth should have seen a copy of those papers. Shouldn't he?

"Didn't you get a copy?" I asked.

Seth looked down, as if embarrassed because he didn't get a copy. For Nobles only, apparently.

"What could they do?" He looked up. "If they were usable."

I shrugged and grabbed the helmet. "Maybe we can blow the thing up." I shrugged again. "I don't know, but I do know we have to do something." I started for the door to the outside. I wanted as much time as possible. Just in case there wasn't anything we could do.

At the threshold I stopped and turned back to Seth, "I'm going to see Quentin and find out about the missiles." He gave me a puzzled look. "Those papers were addressed to him."

Pipe Dreams

Tunnel Vision

I bounced on the seat of the cycle as the engine warmed; the shocks felt stiffer. The exhaust quickly turned the little room into a bakery. I put on my goggles and bolted off the platform.

Back at the CCE Dome, as I was checking out, Joshua informed me that the guide marks in the tunnel had been cleaned off between 'Six and the Ancient City of Tucson. That will help me stay awake.

The drop off at the plateau was coming up in minutes, then it was flat and straight to RS-7. The real fun came between 'Seven and the West Coast, every few kilometers something, and without guide marks.

Two minutes to the drop, I start the pendulum.

With no weave marks to guide me, I start up the left side, focusing on the bend at the end of my headlights. Thoughts of slapping Quentin try to enter my concentration as I pendulum past the amber lights. Pervasions of Alina slip in behind the jettisoned Quentin. I push them out before they catch, my tunnel vision adrenaline fed.

Just as I reached the downward bend, I go up the right side of the pipe. A gentle kiss on the top - perfect. I drop down the left wall, twisting the throttle once on the bottom to keep me there. The speedometer pushes past the scale. I do love it.

I knew I couldn't hit the bend at the bottom going this speed, but waited before easing up, applying the brakes hard just before going up the side. Up and around again. Only once this time, settling quickly. I really do love it.

Level, I push the cycle to the maximum and lock the throttle. I needed a nap. I had roughly ninety minutes. The rhythm of the cycle abetted a quick slip into a trance. Controlled sleep. Subliminal.

Quentin haunted my floating consciousness. In replays of memories, his voice sounds like the cycle engine. He too, like Alina, exhibits reminders of the Apocalypse, except his isn't his hair. Quentin's eyes are clear, transparent. The outlines of his pupil are thin and dark, an opaque cloud hovering within. The iris' are absent and you can see the back of his eye sockets and all the blood vessels in between through the clear eyes.

I was ten when I first met Quentin. He was traveling with a Historian back then, a man named Gunther. They were passing through our village on their way to a new find. Father took a liking to Gunther.

My mother has clear hair, which is probably why I noticed Alina. My hair is black like my father's. My fingers are webbed like his, too.

The group had stopped to ask my father questions and when Quentin removed his hat to be polite, his eyes were unshadowed. I screamed. I had never seen clear eyes. He hasn't liked me since.

When he assumed the responsibility as Head of Tunnel Maintenance twelve years ago he learned to tolerate my presence. I actually kind of like the guy. Although it is rough sometimes when he does something stupid; like have the pipe cleaned. But he will know something about the missiles. Alina will know if they can do anything.

My mind went blank as I tried to picture the rock silently slipping through space towards us; tried to imagine what would happen if it hits; tried to force it to miss.

The reverberation of a cycle engine filtered into the vacuum of space. A voice, an octave lower than the engine, whispered from the darkness of my mind, 'Impossible. Sound doesn't travel in a vacuum.' Would an explosion? Was this futile?

Alina's face filled the void behind my eyes. Her hair was vibrating, humming, the muffled scream of a cycle engine. No, this wasn't useless. Any chance to survive and be with her was worth it. But I should be with her now, let somebody else run the tunnels. But nobody else knows about the missiles. Quentin does. But does he know about the asteroid? He should, the Ancient City of Tucson has two observatories. Perhaps there is a Rider in the other pipe heading to 'Atlanta now. Perhaps.

I have to do this. Push myself a little while longer. Soon I'll be back with Alina, at the edge of the plateau watching the sky, waiting for a flash.

I fell into the drone of the engine, my mind pulling up distant memories.

My father, an archeologist, would leave after each harvest, bringing back grand tales of past deeds. 'Cept it was only me that thought they were grand. They seemed to bring sadness to my father, though at the time I didn't understand why.

After I had become a Rider and before losing that first bag, Father came home extremely upset after a search. He and his team had found the reason for the Apocalypse.

..."I can't believe we're related to those idiots." Father was yelling to Mother, who always stood her ground. It was great fun to watch.

"I can. Look at the way you're acting," Mother said calmly, her arms crossed in annoyance with Father.

Father calmed down a bit after the verbal slap. "Do you know why they blew themselves up?" He knew she didn't, he and his team had just discovered why.

Mother shook her head slowly, a slight 'Tsk' mocking Father.

"Over oil! Can you believe that?!!" He was riled back up. "With all the other ways to generate power they nearly destroyed the planet over that black poison."

"Now, Colby.." Mother tried to interrupt, but Father was on a roll.

"And I do mean *destroy the planet*. The idiots.."

"I do wish you would quit calling our ancestors idiots in front of Benjamin."

Father looked at me and paused. I nodded, just slightly. Father turned back to Mother, and with a finger pointing at me said, "The boy knows their idiots. He works with Quentin."

I coughed out a quick laugh, covering my mouth with my fist.

"The idiots blew up the oil fields!" Father yelled, knowing the neighbors couldn't hear. Quieter, he continued, "Childish. Just childish. When the supply ran low and the countries that had it didn't want to share anymore, the one's without blew up the ones that did. In the process, they blew up the oil fields. Set 'em aflame. Started the whole chain reaction tha..."

Mother stepped forward and kissed Father, effectively shutting him up. She withdrew and said, "You know as well as

I that they went crazy from those cathode raymonds everybody used."

"Cathode ray *tubes*, Roxanne. Not raymonds. And it was radio waves in general. All of 'em. Their antennas on the hill tops and the microwaves from the satellites. Those video and audio signals they beamed all over the planet. All of it cooked their brains."

Father looked over at me, then back to Mother. "Do you think they're right about the cycle riders?"

"No!" I yelled at the gauges. I blinked open my eyes, the shallow glow of the gauges out of focus. I raised only my head and looked down the pipe. I missed my parents.

RS-7

The platform at RS-7 could hold ten cycles. There were three when I pulled in. RS-7 is one of the larger Run-Stops with eighteen domes. Big as it is, my stay was going to be short.

After I gave the man at the CCE counter, Krhyl, their copy of the wonderful news, I trotted over to the Rider complex; three interconnected, five meter domes.

I found two of the Riders, Zachary and Sebastion, complaining about the pipe cleaning. Sebastion told me that Nancy, the third Rider, was in the shower, and that Jay, an eighteen year-old rookie, left thirty minutes ago, headed west. They all knew about the pipe cleaning, but stared in disbelief when I informed them about the asteroid. They laughed when I asked for someone to ride to 'Tucson, so I could head back to

Pipe Dreams

'Six. They wanted to get back to their loved ones.

I needed to be going. I walked out of the dome without a gesture and headed for the CCE Dome.

Krhyl handed the bags back as I passed the counter. I bid him a quick farewell as I snatched a hunk of roasted rabbit from his plate on the counter, eating in the archway to the platform.

Jay

Fifteen minutes into the run from RS-7, as I looped through the third turn, I saw, while upside down, what was left of Jay. His cycle was at the end of my lights. Instinctively I increased throttle, leaning to the gauges.

I crossed the bottom a breath away from the downed cycle and was on the top over most of the debris. I stopped the cycle with squealing tires.

I gasped for air, feeling as though the wind had been knocked out of me. The air tasted of burnt rubber and blood, the rubber the stronger of the two.

Sixty seconds passed before I regained enough to turn off the cycle. I laid the cycle down and walked back through the debris to Jay.

I nearly vomited when I reached his remains. He laid face up, kinda. He was on his back. His neck had been broken and ripped, his head folded under his back. His legs were twisted and tangled together, both arms wrenched from their shoulder sockets and crossed unnaturally over his chest. I closed my eyes and they snapped back open, having to see the blood ooze out of the jagged throat wound just a little longer.

This is the second time I've come across a Rider spread along the pipe. We hear about some old Rider going down every year. It was always difficult to hear about a fellow Rider painting the walls, even worse to find the wet paint.

I suddenly didn't want to ride anymore. I wanted the asteroid to strike now, here at this exact spot, this exact moment.

I walked back to my cycle and put a hand against the tunnel wall to steady myself. I shut my eyes, trying to push them into my head with the lids. What was wrong with me? I wasn't ever, ever, going to paint these stoic walls. I'm too good. I've been riding for fifteen years without an accident. I have an asteroid to stop. I have Alina waiting for me, a lifetime to live together. No, I wasn't ever going to paint the walls.

I straddled the cycle, starting the engine as I adjusted my position.

The Ancient City of Tucson

The Ancient City of Tucson had been spared much of the wrath of the Apocalypse. The ice, too, had spared this dead, ugly city of our ancestors. A lot of the extravagant buildings still stand. A tribute to their ability to build soulless structures. Few today occupy the remaining structures; they are either too hot or too cold, and too inefficient to do anything about either condition.

The archeologists, my father included, have to yet find a purpose for these cities, other than a contempt for nature. The cities apparently did nothing but consume resources and spawn nothing but waste.

Almost nothing. Now, the Ancient City of Tucson and the other few cities left from that time are where we get most of our technology. Fortunately, we use very little of what we uncover; finding it either detrimental to life in general, or useless. Many think it was the belief in their deity, Economy, that led them to technology. It was this belief that caused such disregard for Nature and her resources. From the volumes of literature found on Economy, we believe it was a powerful religion.

Quentin believes that humans have always been, and always will be, insane. He even predicts that in the future, we will once again kill our neighbor. I hope he's wrong. I hope we've outgrown all that nonsense. But, we may not get the chance to prove ourselves.

That rock was falling, pulled towards us by our own planet's gravity. Alina thinks the asteroid is from a ring of the critters that lies past the next planet out. She doesn't know what pushed it from its orbit and towards us, but suspects it has been in a collapsing, spiraling orbit for some years. It has been the source of spectacular, biannual meteor displays whose intensity has increased with each showing. I have seen several: the sky clawed by choreographed star dust with random precision, the night nearly as bright as day. They are intoxicating.

I shot through the exit at 'Tucson faster than we're suppose to, painting a straight snake of black rubber on the concrete deck, the squeal filling the large, rectangular room, reverberating back on itself. Overhead, a transparent peaked roof let in the last of the days light. I parked my cycle by the other four waiting quietly near the CCE door.

Pipe Dreams

As I gather the bags I surmise that with these four Riders here, I'll be free to return to Alina. I push on the door that's labeled pull.

I was exhausted, sore, thirsty, and we were all running out of time. I displaced with the amenities.

"Where's Quentin?" I demanded from Casey, throwing the bags at her hard enough to miss the counter and hit the wall behind it. The others in the room gasped in unison. I knew them. I ignored them and glared at Casey, waiting.

Casey bent down and retrieved the bags, putting them on the counter before meeting my eyes. She, like me, has webbed fingers. "Let me check you in first, before you go running of-."

I kicked the front of the counter, rocking it. "Where is Quentin?!" I heard a chair scoot behind me. Then Walter, a dome builder, was hollering at me.

"Hey there! You just calm down. This is un-"

I spun around on my heel. Walter also had clear eyes and I tried to climb inside them.

"-necessary," he finished, then sat back down without me saying a word. Funny thing is, Walter is bigger than me. I must have looked pretty determined. I turned back to Casey with the same look of determination. I hoped. I was awfully tired.

She smiled, her red hair brushing her cheeks, her emerald green eyes making me feel silly. "Quentin's in the library." Her voice was calm, pleasant. "Have a bad ride, Ben?"

I had forgotten about Jay, until then. With my death looming in the dwindling future, his was quickly buried. I relaxed, slumping to the counter, head in my hands, elbows on the fibre board top. My eyes stared unfocused on the bottom of the CCE bags. "Jay is dead," I whispered coarsely. Casey sucked in a mouthful of air, I went on with the details. "'Bout ten, fifteen minutes out of 'Seven. Just past turn three. He must not have been going fast enough and just.." I paused, seeing the body again. "He wasn't going fast enough and just dropped of the top."

    Water, in a wooden goblet, was placed on the counter in front of me. Casey's webbed hand withdrew, but not before giving the top of my head a gentle caress. She use to clean up the paint jobs us Riders leave every once and a while before being promoted to her current position. She knew what I had seen; knew that I nearly did a paint job myself because of the mess.

    "I'm sorry, Benjamin. I know it was bad."

I took the goblet and gulped the water.

"I'll get a crew out there right away."

I held up the empty goblet. "Thanks."

    I felt everyone's eyes on me as I headed for the door to the outside. I know they didn't hear what I told Casey about Jay. I did feel bad for coming in the way I did. Casey would apologize for me.

    Outside the air was chilly, I could smell the warm concrete of the city and the salty water from the coast. The sun was past the horizon, its loom illuminating the city streets with a ghostly, pale red light. It was one kilometer to the library. I started walking. A few steps later I was running, the ten centimeter heels used to catch the pegs of the cycle forcing the sole to the pavement with an echoing slap. I stopped and removed my boots. Then, a boot in each hand, I started running again.

The carvings and sculptures on the outside walls of the library are all but wiped away by erosion. Three windows high, it held a presence of cold and echoes.

I slowed when the door came into view, winded, sucking in air by the lung full. My feet were numb. Sweat slid down my face, back and hands. It felt good, my body pulsing with life. The missiles had to work. They just had to.

I found Quentin on the second level, a wide balcony that encircled the first floor. He was sitting at a small table by the railing. Splayed out before him were several books. A shaded oil lamp lighted the cluster. He watched as I approached, curious. I usually don't seek him out.

"Benjamin," he said as I plopped down in the chair across from him. "What are you doing here?" He wasn't upset, but, then again, he wasn't all that delighted, either.

"Nice to see you, too, Quentin. We have a problem."

Quentin sighed. "You're not going to complain about the paint, are you? I thought you guys would appreciate it."

He was serious. I had to ask. "Did you ask a Rider about the marks before you decided to have them cleaned off?"

Quentin shook his head. I rolled my eyes. I wanted to slap him, but there wasn't time. "You do know about the rock hurling towards us?"

He nodded.

"I need to know about the nuclear missiles."

"How.." he started, then I saw the realization as he remembered back. He leaned forward, putting an elbow on the table and pointed a finger at me. "You did read those papers."

I nodded, smug. "And quite a few since then."

He tsk'd with disgust. "We're suppose to be able to trust you guys."

"That's what I was going to say."

He glared at me. Quentin is suppose to be one of our elite, a Noble. Information, it was taught in school, is suppose to pass through him, not stopped and dissected. And I knew the missiles were not the only data withheld by Quentin. Yet I still kinda liked him, though I wouldn't trust him to top off the tank.

"I need to know about the missiles." I leaned forward, putting my elbows on the table, then noticed the books. They were on astronomy. "We have a little over a day to do something. The missiles. How many?"

"Seventeen." Quentin looked at me, the blood vessels in the clear whites obscuring the back. "I thought the Star Gazers here had erred. But you say there is an asteroid coming for us." He was dumbfounded. No, shocked. "I had hoped deeply that they had erred."

"The missiles, Quentin."

"They won't do any good. Besides, we need to contact the other Nobles and have a meet-"

I slapped the table top, hard. My hand screamed with hot pain as I yelled at Quentin, "We don't have the time for nobility!" I retracted my hand, hoping he didn't notice the pain in my eyes. I laid it in my lap, then stated more civil, "The missiles need to be used. Who do we contact?"

"Gunther." My fit of rage didn't persuade him to tell me. A fear had entered Quentin, I could see it in his clear eyes. Impending death. His own.

I left Quentin as he mumbled about Star Gazers and the margin of error.

Pipe Dreams

The Flight Back

When I arrived back at CCE I discovered that the four Riders that were there had left. There was no one to tell Gunther to launch the missiles, except me.

I mounted my cycle. Casey had seen that it was serviced. Her I trusted. I started the engine, letting it warm a moment as I adjusted zippers, crotch and goggles, then shot down the dock and into the eastbound tunnel. I sped up the incline, looping 'round the top at the top.

The tunnels ran roughly parallel, going their own way at some of the more rugged landscapes, but always coming back and connecting at the Run-Stops. Just past the first curve the eastbound starts on its own course through the mountainous terrain separating 'Tucson and RS-7. It comes adjacent to the westbound tunnel again five minutes outside 'Seven.

I reach the first curve and slide up the left wall as I veer right, up past the amber lights, my head pointed slightly toward the bottom. I was flying, keeping the cycle near top speed as I whipped through the first set of curves, zipping around the top out of each. On the straight away I twisted the throttle until it stopped, laying down on the tank, peeking over the gauges. Time was ticking away, slipping away, falling away. I concentrated on riding, on the pipe ahead, on getting to Alina. I slipped into a zone. Fifteen years I've ran these tunnels; tired as I was, I had to trust myself.

There was one cycle when I arrived back at RS-7. Krhyl was still at the counter, although he looked terribly sad.

Pipe Dreams

"I can't believe it's going to hit," he said when I entered.

"Maybe they're wrong and it'll miss us," I mused.

There was a brightening in his eyes, on his face. Not much, but I had given him the idea of a chance, a hope.

I looked around the dome, then turned back to Krhyl. "Where's the Rider? Over at berthing?"

Krhyl shook his head, "Nope. It's Montgomery. He went home."

I slammed my fist down on the counter, "Damn!"

"What?" Krhyl timidly asked.

I almost told him about the missiles, but thought against it. There wasn't time to explain. "Somebody needs to ride to the east coast," was all I said as I walked away. Still, before I dragged myself out the door, I hinted for him to watch the sky for a flash.

I had ninety minutes of straight away again. I locked the throttle, then hesitated before putting my head down. This tired, would I wake up in time?

Somebody will be at 'Six to pass the information to Gunther. No nap. I'll wait until I'm with Alina. Time to stay awake. I unlocked the throttle, then re-locked it and let go the grips.

Leaning into the wind, my arms down and slightly out, thighs tight against the cycle, I fly. Balanced on two, small, rubber pads less than a meter above a blurry death, I fly. Through a pipe four meters wide, zoned with the hum of the cycle, my tunnel vision complete, I fly.

Pipe Dreams

Alina

There are no cycles on either platform at RS-6, but I couldn't go on. The cycle needed fuel and the lubricant changed. I needed to find Alina. Then, somehow, go on. Somehow those missiles were going to work, even if they had to scare the asteroid away.

The CCE Dome was empty when I arrived. I found Alina with her father at home. Seth looked defeated, as exhausted as I felt. Alina had been crying again, her eyes puffy and red. I received the distinct impression that things had somehow gotten worse.

Still, tired as I was, achy and sore as I was, I was excited about the missiles. We were saved, or at least had a chance.

"...There's seventeen. All working," my words were quick, short, and directed at Alina.

She looked at me, sad eyes asking why. "The missiles won't work."

I blinked. It was joke. "Why not?"

"There are no explosions in outer space, Benjamin. There's no air for the concussion to travel through." Alina was serious. "We can't do anything to it."

I rolled my eyes, "They won't blow it up?"

"No."

This was ridiculous. Humanity survives its own attempt at destroying the world, lives through the aftermath, and now is going to get wiped out by a kid throwing rocks in space. "We've got to be able to do something."

Pipe Dreams

Alina shrugged. "I wish there was, Benjamin. But I don't see how your missiles will do any good."

I stared at her dumbfounded. Had she given up, too? Had she given up on us? "They're all we have. We have to try." I moved one step closer to her, "I want more time with you. I'll do anything for that chance."

"Even if it means being without me now?" The need for my presence thick on her breath.

"I have to try," was all I could come up with.

"Do we know where it's going to hit?" I looked at Seth with the question.

"Somewhere south of 'Two. Probably in the water." His tone was that of someone reporting a fact, a fact with no consequence to the messenger.

"It'll wipe out the entire east side, from 'Atlanta to RS-4," Alina added, talking to the floor. "It could put us in another ice age, blocking out the sun with all the debris it'll kick up."

I stood there, trying to imagine living in continuous darkness. No stars, no moon, the sun a dull disc obscured by thick smoke and dust. It would be worse than the tunnels. I sulked with this thought for a few moments. Was there nothing we could do but wait? The missiles had to be able to do something? Even if it was only to break the asteroid into smaller pieces, wouldn't that save us from another ice age?

"How much longer?" I asked.

"About thirty-one hours," Alina said, then asked, "Why, Benjamin?"

"The missiles," I blurted. "If we break it up into smaller chunks, will it still cause an ice age?"

Alina looked to Seth. Seth turned to me and said, "We

don't have the authority to do something like that, Benjamin. That could cause wide spread destruction."

"And what do you call another ice age? Winter?!" I was too tired for this. I needed help, support, not arguments. "We don't have the time to run back and forth through the tunnels getting the authority, either," I pointed out, then turned to Alina. "I need anything you can tell me about the asteroid."

"It's all at the observatory."

Even horses were too slow for that trip. We would take the cycle. "Seth," I barked as I snapped my head to him. I wasn't going to give up. And they were going to help. "I need my cycle outside." We've had cycles outside before, for emergencies at outlying villages.

"What for?" Seth contested. I was waiting for the, 'It's no use' that followed, but he remained silent. I lost my temper anyway.

"I have to get to the observatory and collect what I can carry about that damn rock for Gunther.

"Then I have to make it to Gunther's, then I have to get Gunther to launch the missiles, without the proper authorization. Now get somebody to get my cycle into the archway!" I spun and walked out the door to the outside. I stood in the center of the yard and looked to the distant hills, lost in anger.

Alina joined me a minute or so later. "Father says he'll need your help with the cycle. Everyone else is at home. Waiting."

I sighed. I was too tired to go on. "Let's go." As we headed back to the dome, I said, "You're going for a cycle ride, you know."

"I had that impression. I can't wait. But what a reason."

"Speaking of waiting..,"

"I know," Alina interrupted. "We'll have to get married when you get back."

With the cycle in the archway that led to the CCE Dome and Alina waiting outside, I asked Seth for another favor.

"Seth?" I was astride the cycle, ready to start it.

"Hmm?"

"I need you to go to the Hermit while I'm at the observatory."

"What for?" he asked, surprised.

"Coca leaves. I'm dead, but I can't give up. I need to keep going."

Hesitantly he agreed. "I'll get them. Anything else?"

I thought a moment, then added, "A map showing an outside route to 'Atlanta is all else I can think of."

"It'll be here. You be careful with my daughter on this thing." He slapped the back fender. "Now get outta here."

I started the cycle, then looked back at Seth. "Want a ride?"

Alina was laughing as her father and I pulled up to her in the yard outside the CCE Dome. "You should have seen Father's eyes, Benjamin. He was sca..."

"That'll be enough, Alina," Seth commanded as he dismounted.

It was nice to see her smiling, but we were fighting time, a meticulous foe. "Get on," I told her.

"Yes, sir," she teased and climbed on with a smile.

When she was on the cycle behind me, holding me

around the waist, I turned my head and whispered, "I'm sorry for yelling."

"I know," she said. "Now drive."

The moon was rising behind us, a big, bright moon. I haven't ridden outside the tunnel in years, and Seth was my first passenger. Alina felt good behind me, her body pressed against mine, her grip tight. She was doing well, considering this was a first for her too. I toyed with the idea of taking her with me to find Gunther, but after the first rut I realized any passenger would slow me down too much. Traveling outside is going to do that as it is, but both tunnels will be filled with people coming this way. I'll never make it through. I'll have to ride outside.

At the observatory Alina ran in to get her papers while I idled with the cycle just outside the door. All I could think about was cuddling up with Alina and falling asleep. Just sleep. Sleep until the asteroid did its thing.

We took it just as quick on the way back, Alina holding on tightly, quietly.

The moon was higher now, illuminating the desert to a grey level. Close to the horizon was the faint glow of the asteroid. It didn't look that ominous of a light. 'Six was back-lit by the moon, black silhouettes against a clear, starry sky.

Gifts from the Hermit

Seth was sitting in a simple chair by the front door to the Riders dome, watching the asteroid, something smoldering in his hand. I circled the yard and headed straight for him, the headlights beaming in his face. He raised his hand to shield his eyes. When I shut the cycle down he dropped his hand from his eyes and raised the other one to his mouth, inhaling from the rolled paper.

"What are you doing, Father?" Alina was indignant, her tone as if her father were a child. Smoking was as bad as radio waves. She slid off the cycle and marched the few steps to him, sniffing at the air. She stood just to his left, a meter or so in front of him, hands on her hips, waiting for his reply.

Seth let the smoke roll off his lip and up his face as he exhaled with the control of a saxophone player. He watched the smoke rise in the moonlight, eyes darting to Alina now and again. He puffed out what was in his lungs and straightened his posture. "The Hermit said it would help me accept the inevitable. Tastes wonderful." He inhaled more smoke from the paper tube, raising his free hand to me, a leather pouch the size of his palm dangling from his fingers. "Here," he said through clenched teeth.

Alina stepped over in a huff and snatched the smoking tube from her father's hand. "You've had enough," she scolded.

I kicked out the side-stand and dismounted, walked over and took the bag from Seth's extended hand. "Coca leaves?" I asked.

Seth nodded. "Hermit says to chew 'em until there's nothing left to chew," he reached under the chair to pick up a scroll. "Says you shouldn't need more than two to get you to the coast. There's a handful in there, so go easy with 'em." He handed me the scroll. It was a map.

"I've marked the quickest route; open paths beside the tunnels mostly. I figure you can run the pipe until 'Four, maybe even 'Three. Doubt if you'll even be able to run the paths by the pipes past 'Two, though. I marked a by-pass route for you starting at 'Four, just in case."

I took the scroll and looked at it in the moonlight.

"I've been sitting here watching that rock fall for quarter of an hour now." Seth rambled on with filler. "It's actually kinda pretty, the tiny tail and all."

Alina and I looked over our shoulders. It did have a tail.

"Been thinking about how maybe somebody out there don't like us. Somebody in a spaceship or something. From a different world. They pushed that asteroid," he pointed to the eastern sky, "towards us."

I smiled. I knew he couldn't see my face with the moon behind me. "And why would they do that, Seth?"

He turned to me, staring at my eyes. "Because we still haven't got it right." I couldn't see his eyes, either, but I felt them. I stopped smiling.

"Got what right, Father?" Alina asked.

"Living on this planet. We're still doing something wrong."

I couldn't help it, I laughed. I meant no harm, but I still felt Seth shrink. I stopped laughing and composed myself best I could. My legs felt like rubber.

I opened the leather bag and removed a leaf. I placed the leaf in my mouth and started chewing. The taste was awful, bitter, causing me to shake my head involuntarily. Then there was a flush, something rushing over me, through me. Suddenly I felt refreshed, revitalized.

I walked over to Seth and put my hand on his shoulder,

catching a whiff of what he was smoking. It had a wonderful, alluring aroma.

"I didn't mean to laugh, Seth. I'm just exhausted."

Seth sucked in air, trying to swallow my apology. "Yeah," he drawled out.

"Maybe somebody did push that rock towards us, but we haven't done anything wrong, Seth. Nothing we do harms our world. I don't think that's what it is."

"Then what?" he challenged.

I shrugged, "Just Nature fucking with us."

Alina gasped. Seth giggled. "I can accept that," he said.

I kissed Alina. "See you soon," I whispered, then went to the cycle, smiling. I felt good. Exhilarated. I mounted the cycle and looked at Seth. He was right, I probably can run the pipe to 'Four, but he was in no condition to help me get the cycle back in the tunnel.

"Isn't there anybody around that could help me load this into the pipe?" I asked him.

Seth swiped his smoke back from his daughter with deft ease. He drew from the burning tube, then explained,

"The map shows an old ramp about half a kilometer west of here. Guess they used it during construction of the tunnel, but I think your cycle will fit through the opening." He drew again on the smoke, then added, "The Hermit said to make it skip."

Alina came over when I lowered my goggles, putting her arms around my shoulders. "Hurry back," she whispered.

I kissed her quickly on the lips. "Back before the big bang." I put the cycle in gear. Alina backed away as I released the clutch. The rear tire kicked up dirt. I was off, with thirty hours until impact.

The remark Seth had echoed from the Hermit rolled around in my head, *make it skip*. Make what skip? Why didn't I ask? I drove by instinct, the leaf in my mouth assisting the process as *make it skip* ricocheted and echoed inside my skull.

Minutes later, *make it skip* still unanswered, I spotted the ramp. I had to get off the cycle to open the access panel, but I could ride through the opening. I left the access panel open, heading down the tunnel as fast as the cycle would go.

I ripped through a curve, zinging around the pipe in a dizzying swoop. My mind shifted and I was watching Mom and Dad again.

"They wiped out entire peoples for their land. Sometimes just because they looked different." Father was furious, his tone of venomous accusations. He had returned from another search, with another discovery about our ancestors.

"*You* look different when you're angry," Mother tried to muse. When Father only glowered, Mother asked in her usual calm voice, "How did they look different?" Trying to understand Father's rage.

"Before the Apocalypse, people were of different races."

"There was more than one human race?" Mother questioned.

"No." Father was quieter now, calmer. He was explaining. "Just different varieties of people from what we can find. Skin color was a little variant, but the papers we found were written with hate. It doesn't make sense."

"Radio Wave Madness," Mother offered.

Pipe Dreams

Father shrugged. "Evidence says they were doing it long before radio waves ever filled the air."

Another curve, another swoop. I swallowed the leaf mulch. Again, my mind shifted. I was with Alina.

We were several kilometers north of my home village. Alina was laying on a hemp blanket, watching as I skipped stones across the glass on top the lake.

"You're father doesn't like what he does, does he?" she asked.

Another flat stone kissed the water and skipped, once, twice, four times. "Sure he does. That's why he chose it. He just doesn't always like what he finds." Another stone, two skips.

"Why doesn't he stop, do something else?"

I threw another stone, watching it skip six times, before passing on what my father told me what he was searching for.

"He told me after I started running the pipe that he wanted to find all the good that he could from the past."

She shifted, rolling onto her side, facing me. "How much has he found?"

Another stone was sent to the depths of the lake after spending eons to crawl out. "How much what?"

"Good things?"

"So far?" Another stone humiliated in four skips.

"Yes, so far."

"Not much." Another stone, thrown side-armed into the lake, skips on the atmosphere of the planet; once, twice, thrice! Then tumbles hopelessly towards the sun.

I jerked and the cycle wobbles for an instant. My vision is fuzzy. The amber lights of the tunnel bright; I was looking down a lit V etched in blur.

I shake my head hard in an attempt to clear my sight, then readjust my goggles and look down the tunnel. The blur isn't as bad, but the lights are still bright. They hurt, causing me to squint. It was better the other way. I slide my fingers under the goggles and rub my eyes. My head feels fluid, my eyes floating balls.

Whoa.

Slowly I raise my eyelids, my arms and the handlebars focus in. I open my eyes all the way and the tunnel is normal, clear, in focus, just the lights are bright. This was more than exhaustion. The leaves I were chewing had to be a cause for some of this. I did feel awake, though. Very awake. The dream, though, was gone. Forgotten.

Eastward Bound

'Five was empty, not even the operator was there. I fueled the cycle myself, popped another leaf in my mouth, and shot down the pipe, desperately needing this to be over. I was pushing myself and the cycle. In the twenty or so minutes I spent searching 'Five, the cycle cooled only slightly. I haven't slept, other than the naps on the cycle, in roughly thirty-six hours.

But the worst part was that no one wanted to help. A collective defeatism had seized the populace. I couldn't comprehend their complacency, their resignation. After all we've accomplished in the hundred and thirty some years since the ice started to recede, everyone was just giving up. I chewed the leaf vigorously, anger seeping in with the bitter juice towards the unknowing cowards.

Then it struck me, they must not know about the missiles. If they did, there would be hope, and support. I wouldn't be racing across the land dead tired, if there was support. I couldn't find fault with them though. If it wasn't for the missiles and the possibility that they'll be affective, I would be huddled somewhere with Alina, waiting for the end.

A hostility sparked, directed at those who knew about the missiles and stayed silent. I scolded myself for not having said something all those years ago, nipping my tongue as I chewed even quicker. Then realized that if we had known about the missiles years ago, they would no doubt be dismantled now.

I pushed the thoughts down, forcing my agitated mind on the tunnel, wanting the next curve sooner than the two minutes.

Four hours had passed since leaving RS-6 and I was still eight hours from 'Atlanta. I had just left RS-4. I didn't go in search of anyone this time; people were trickling down both tunnels as I refueled the cycle, from as far away as RS-1. I knew a few of them, more than I would have imagined. Several helped me put the cycle outside.

The moon was behind me as I headed east. Crawling over the horizon in front of me was Orion. The asteroid was almost directly overhead, its tail now a little bit longer. It was starting to look ominous. Up and over my left shoulder was the eastbound tunnel, next to it the westbound. The air was cool, crisp; it stung my face as I flew down the wide, dirt path; the flora increasing on both sides. I wished Alina was behind me now, squeezing tight. I was suddenly very lonely.

After all my years of running the tunnels solo; spending most of my time in solitude when not riding; now, as certain death glowed above, I longed for the company of only one.

I rode, seeing pairs of red eyes filled with fright stare from the thickening bush. Then an insect, approximately the size of a fly judging from the splatter, hit me in the goggles.

I had forgotten about the bugs. The suddenness surprised me and I licked my lips of the splatter. I wiped the guts off my goggles, then lowered my face to the gauges, scooting my butt back as far as I could until the wind was blowing over me. Insects still struck the top of my head, but I wouldn't be eating anymore. I chewed the remains of the leaf with lips closed.

I rode like that to RS-3, slaloming between tunnel supports and dodging the occasional pedestrian without raising from my stance. From 'Three to 'Two the foot traffic increased until there was a blur of people on both sides of the path.

At RS-2 I was told that no one was in the tunnel, everyone was walking outside to watch the oncoming rock. That sounded good, but I did not want to be going top speed and run into somebody walking in the tunnel. As I was refueling the cycle, Yvonne, an operator at RS-1, stopped briefly for a visit.

The Tunnel Access Platform is just a meter off the ground here, a short ramp allowing access. I stood by the valve at the gravity tank, the hose stuck in the cycle's fuel tank, waiting for the hose to move, the signal it was time to shut-off the valve.

"Is there room for two on that thing?" Yvonne said from behind. "I saw you come in," she said, the door to the outside clicked shut behind her.

I didn't look away from the cycle as I replied, "I'm headed east."

"What?!" Her surprise was loud.

"You heard," I was too tired for politeness, and busy. The hose jerked. The level was close to the top. I wheeled the valve shut to a dribble and topped off the tank. I hung up the hose, then stepped over to the cycle.

"Why, Ben?" Yvonne was shocked, stunned. "Is someone back there hurt?"

"No," I said as I secured the fuel cap.

"Then, why?"

I mounted the cycle, then turned to Yvonne. "I heard there was no one using the tunnels. Is that true?"

Yvonne nodded. "Only the eastbound. We heard news about the west headed this way." She looked at the satchel laying on my back, the strap running around my neck and under an arm. "Is that what you're carrying? What is it?"

"There may be some hope." I started the engine as she said, 'What?'. I didn't hear it, but it was easy to read her lips. I shrugged, blew her a kiss, then darted into the tunnel.

*   *   *

Thirty minutes later, as I settle at the bottom after coming off the top, I spot a small, dark silhouette ahead. My heart kicks my chest and I stop breathing. It's a person! A child! There was no time to stop.

He came into my beam a moment later, eyes in

shocked terror, his mouth open to a scream I couldn't hear. Graciously, he was scared stiff. Still targets are easier to miss.

Back and forth I swooped in on the boy, the seconds it took to reach him seemed hours long. Repeatedly I fought visions of running into him *head* on. I had to concentrate on the maneuver. My legs ached from squeezing the tank, my knuckles straining to hold on tighter. I'm going to miss...I'm going to miss...I'm going to miss.

Two meters in front of the boy I cross from one wall to the other, leaning into the fall and stretching the throttle cable. Up and around I pass him. Down behind him I slide, the momentum pushing me up and around again. I ease off the throttle and pendulum on the bottom.

I wanted to stop and see about the boy, but knowing I had missed, I pushed on, hoping his parents weren't up ahead. But as I strained to see the possible silhouettes at the end of my beam, I couldn't stop thinking about how frightened that little boy must be. I couldn't stop feeling guilty, neither.

I didn't come across his parents, nor anyone else, but the little boy haunted me until I reached 'Atlanta.

The Ancient City of Atlanta

I reached the Ancient City of Atlanta without further incident. At the CCE center I got the cycle back outside with ease. It sat on its side-stand as I stretched my legs.

The sun was bright and climbing towards midmorning as I drank water and looked at the map. Gunther's home was another hour away. The streets were empty. I had not seen anyone since the little boy in the tunnel.

The Ancient City of Atlanta thrilled me about as much as Tucson, the structures just as ugly, but I wasn't staying long. I mounted the cycle and continued my solitary trek as I headed north out of the city.

The sound of the cycle is different in the city. Out in the open the voice of the cycle is underneath and behind me, pushed down and back by the force of the wind. In the tunnel the sound surrounds and engulfs me. But inside the city the sound has time to rumble between the buildings, fading out where another street crosses.

It gave me an odd feeling when I realized that this is where my ancestors rode their cycles. Here, on this very street. I wondered for some time where they could have been going.

When I could see hills unmarred by ancient buildings I realized I would be out of the city soon. Suddenly I could not wait to be outside the city, the asteroid, for the moment, forgotten. Instead, my thoughts were riding the open country. There was something about riding outside the pipe and the cities that caused my spirits to rise.

The cool morning air feels good in my hair. Holding the throttle with my left hand, I unzip the left wrist, then do the same for the right arm and a few inches at the neck. I was chewing the leaf I started at 'One.

Gunther's

An eternity later, about twenty minutes, I was past the last ugly, ancient building, headed down a narrow path through a meadow of tall grass. The meadow, a grain field, unfurled to the horizon. Somewhere further on was Gunther and the missiles.

Thirty minutes later I crested a small rise and stopped. Across the shallow valley, on the top of the next hill was a single small dome with no windows. I checked the map. It had to be Gunther's.

As I raced down the gentle slope I wondered where the missiles were; I couldn't even see a tree within ten kilometers. Perhaps they were on the other side of the next hill.

Reaching the hill with the dome didn't solve the sudden mystery; there still wasn't any missiles to be seen. The sun was crossing noon and the land on this side was grassy and flat to the forest on the horizon. Another tree line was in the haze of distance to the north, a gradual slope down to the south. I stopped the cycle several meters from the dome entrance and set it on its center-stand, then had a disturbing thought - What if Gunther wasn't home?

I knelt beside the cycle, the engine tinking as it cooled, and cried. I didn't know if he was here or not, it didn't matter. I needed sleep, food, water, and a good cry. I bawled for several minutes, coughing and choking on the phlegm. The wails of exhaustion and anguish rolled across the open land. If Gunther hadn't heard the cycle, he was sure to have heard those.

A nose rattling sniff and a wipe with the back of my hand brought me some composure. I stood, using the cycle to stabilize myself. My knees cracked as I rose, my back ached and my arms were sore. I remained leaning on the cycle seat, my legs straight, bent over at the waist, studying the ground.

The sunny meadow looked inviting, the yellow-green

grain thick and plush. I thought about laying back in the grain and closing my eyes. I could be asleep and have the asteroid hit me. It was tempting. Very tempting.

"That you, Digger?"

I snapped straight, startled. I hadn't heard the door of the dome open, yet in the open doorway stood Gunther, his large, rotund frame filling the opening. He calls me 'Digger' because of father. I know it really doesn't make sense, but it does to him. Besides, he calls my father Colt.

Gunther had been with Quentin when I screamed at the eyes of the latter so long ago. Gunther had laughed at the incident and consequently became friends with my father for a while. He use to visit before he and my father had a falling out a few months before I became a Rider. I didn't know what happened, and no one explained why Gunther quit coming over. In fact, I didn't understand until sixteen hours ago when Quentin told me it was Gunther who could launch the missiles. Father must have found out about the missiles.

I grabbed the document pack containing the information Alina gave me and walked towards him as he stepped through the doorway. We met halfway between my cycle and the dome and shook hands.

"It is you," Gunther said. His bald head gleamed in the sun. "How's that pissy ol' man of yours?" He sounded happy to see me.

"Stuck in the past," I replied, my euphemism to his death.

He pulled me to him, putting his arm around my shoulder. We had not been this close even when he and Father were friends. I believed I was hallucinating from the coca leaves and looked back to the grass beside the cycle, expecting to see myself lying there asleep.

"You did bring the data about the asteroid, didn't you?" Gunther asked, almost joyous with anticipation. "That is why you're here?"

I was stunned at his assessment and it must have shown.

"Don't look so shocked, Digger. I heard you read those papers about the missiles I sent to Quentin way back when. I also know about you and Seth's girl. You were sure to find out about the asteroid. Did it take you long to think about the missiles?"

I shook my head as I pondered how he got his information about me.

"Didn't think it would, you're a smart boy. When I heard about that rock coming our way I knew my missiles were our only hope. I've been expecting you. Did think you'd get here a lot sooner, though."

I have to admit, Gunther is smart, intelligent. He just smells.

"Well..let me see the papers." Gunther danced in place as if he had to go pee, hands out to receive the asteroid information.

I handed him the bag. "It's all inside." As he took the bag and opened it, I looked around.

"Where are the missiles?"

Gunther stopped peeking in the bag and looked out to the low, rolling hills. "They're out there."

Still looking at the landscape I said, "Really."

"Really," Gunther confirmed. "They're in dens. In the

ground. Disguised. We can watch from here when they go up."

"I plan on being on my way back to 'Six by then."

"We'll see. Come."

I followed Gunther back to his dome as he babbled on about how he needed to figure missile trajectory. I tried to follow his muttering but he was talking more to himself than me.

I just wanted to know how soon before he knew if the missiles could do anything, and when? Then I could leave. I had to know before I could leave. Had to.

I thought how I should probably sleep, but I could sleep after I was back with Alina. Little more than ten hours. I pulled out another leaf and put it in my mouth as we entered Gunther's dome.

A single wooden door stood in the center of the dimly lit dome. Several candles illuminated the apse that held the door up.

"What is all this?" I asked.

Gunther opened the door. "My home," he said, then went through the doorway.

I followed him onto a spiral staircase that led down the center of a deep, square shaft, the door closing behind me with a gentle click. A candle burned at each complete twist of the stairs. The air was cool, moist, and smelt of beeswax. The temperature dropped as we descended. I felt I was entering a tomb.

"You live underground?" I was astounded.

"Obviously," he said as we continued downward. "Maybe you're not as smart as I thought you were."

"I've just never seen anybody living underground."

"Once you get use to the lack of windows it's pretty cool. Literally. The temperature hovers around twenty degrees, varying by five degrees from summer to winter, and it's always quiet," Gunther explained. "I've put up some pictures of landscapes I found in the city. They help."

Moments later we passed a walkway to a door as we continued our descent down the twisting, metal stairs, the echoes of our footfalls cascading up and down the shaft into a constant asynchronous rhythm.

"How far down are we going?" I don't know why I sounded nervous. Perhaps because I had never been underground before, perhaps because my father had disliked Gunther.

"All the way to the bottom, thirteen meters."

"What's down there?"

"My shop. We just passed where I live." Gunther stopped and turned so he could face me. "This is part of a missile silo. Built eighty years before the Apocalypse, so you know how old it is."

That's why I was nervous. I was in an underground structure built millennia ago by our ancestors, the ones my father liked to call idiots. "Are you sure it's safe?"

Gunther laughed, his high pitch cackle reverberating in the shaft and my head. "I've been here twenty years. Answer your question." He headed back down the stairs, clumping his weight down hard on the metal grating.

The staircase shook and vibrated. I grabbed for the railing with both hands. "Knock it off, you fat idiot. I don't trust anything they built."

Gunther ceased stomping and turned to me. "You're

going to trust these missiles to work, aren't you?"

I slowly nodded, noticing that Gunther's eyes were wet. I had hurt him when I called him fat. But he was fat. Still, I apologized.

"I'm sorry for calling you fat, Gunther. I was," I paused. "I was scared."

"I'm not an idiot. A bit obese, yes. But not an idiot." Then, just before turning to continue down the stairs, almost as an afterthought, Gunther said, "You've been scared for hours."

We descended with only the symphony of footfalls and the flickering of burning candles. In the final turn before the bottom I had to know,

"Where's the missile that was here?"

Gunther reached the cement floor and stopped, looking up to me. "It was launched during the Apocalypse. Along with nine others they struck a place they called England. What insanity." Then he kicked the staircase, sending a shiver up the metalwork, and me. "They did wonders with concrete and steel, though."

"That's a matter of opinion," I said as I joined him at the bottom.

"What? You don't trust what they built? Look how long their structures have lasted. Look at the pipe you boys zoom through." He was slightly agitated, the volume and pitch rising slightly. "They'll be here long after we're gone."

"Not if the asteroid hits," I reminded him. "And it's not that I don't trust what they built, it's more I don't like looking at the ugly things." Then I noticed there were two doors, on opposing walls. "Now where?"

Gunther moved towards the door behind him, "In

here."

"What's that way?" I asked, meaning the door behind me.

"The other silo. Half full of water now. Door's welded shut." Gunther pulled the thick door open. "My water supply." He pushed the door open wide, kicking a wedge under it after banging the door against the wall. "I've got a telescope over there, too. On a scaffolding near the rim. It's a small one, but I'll be able to watch the explosions." He entered the room, motioning with his hand for me to follow.

I stepped into the round room and into the ancient past. There were more candles and oil lamps illuminating the place with a bright, dancing, natural glow. On both sides of me two heavy tables formed a path between work areas: Equipment to manufacture things, work material, shop tools. I had seen pictures of the machines in books when I was younger, but could only remember a single name, Drill Press. Another heavy table was in front of eleven grey, metal consoles, curved around half the room on the far side, twelve meters away. Dials, switches, gauges and lights neatly cluttered the facades of the equipment. Racks and stacks of metal and cut wood stood guard between the shop tools and grey consoles. All the consoles were on, the little lights blinking and gauge needles twitching. I could hear the hum of current, even from the doorway.

"Where are you getting all the power?"

"From solar panels in the city. Where else?" Gunther sounded disappointed, as though I should have known.

"Solar panels are running these?" I said astonished, waving a hand past the machines.

"It's the only thing they're running." Gunther walked over to a table in front of the grey consoles and laid out the documents from the bag I delivered. Fitting a pair of reading glasses of his own on, he leaned over the papers and studied them with great interest. "Hmm-m-m," he muttered, putting a hand under his chin.

I walked over to the table and Gunther. "What's the 'hmm', hmm-m-m?" I asked, putting my elbows on the table.

"Hmph? Oh, the size of the rock." He read from the paper in front of him, "They think it's oblong, three kilometers at the longest. Tumbling head-over-heels, so to speak. They also think it's made of a metal ore, and not rock. Your girl doesn't think my missiles will be able to do anything."

I maintained my gaze on Gunther, wanting him to look my way so I could watch his eyes. He turned his head when I asked, "Do you?"

Staring back into my eyes, he said, "Can't say without studying the data more." He turned back to the papers. "It being iron, I doubt we can destroy it, even with seventeen missiles. There just isn't the tonnage."

"Tonnage?"

"Explosive power. We just don't have the power to really hurt a thing that size."

I stood up straight. "Oh really. Can we at least deflect it?"

"I doubt it. It's three kilometers long, remember." Gunther looked back at the papers. A moment later he added, "It's half a kilometer thick." He straightened up, walked around the table and over to one of the humming consoles. From the top of the console he removed a clipboard, reading it as he returned to the table. "Maybe ..maybe we can divert it. At least make it skip off the atmosphere."

"That's what the Hermit meant," I burst out, startling Gunther into dropping the clipboard. That is also what the pipe dream was about. I felt like an ancestor - an idiot.

It was obvious he had no idea what I was talking about by his, "What?" as he picked up the clipboard.

"Someone at 'Six mentioned something about making it skip. Now I know what he meant." I was excited. The daydream in the tunnel flashed through my thoughts. "We'll make that damn rock skip off our atmosphere like a stone on a pond. This means it'll work. It has to work."

Gunther was staring at me. "I hope so." He turned back to the table, picked up a pencil and started figuring, now and again checking the documents I brought. He mumbled as he wrote: "Forty thousand kilometers...twelve, no eleven..four thousand.. megatons..minus..times.. minus..."

My mind drifted as I listened to Gunther's rhythmic mathematics. I floated to Alina's observatory, to the edge of the plateau. I sat down beside Alina. She was quiet, her back to the edge, staring east. I felt she was waiting for my return. I needed to leave Gunther's.

"It's going to be close, Digger. Real close."

I shook my head to clear it of Alina and asked the obvious, "How close?" I was still chewing the coca leaf and was beginning to get antsy just standing there. I needed to ride.

Gunther checked his figures, then the time. "It's a little over sixteen hours until impact. The missiles will reach it in eight hours." He looked up from the papers. "Wish it was ten."

"Will they do anything?"

"I wish we had twenty hours and seventeen more missiles." He glanced to the table, then back at me. "We can only hope. Now, I need your help to get them launched."

Help? I wanted to leave, not hang around. I needed to ride. But what good the ride if it is cut short by falling rocks? "What can I do to help?"

Over the next thirty minutes Gunther and I entered trajectory coordinates and launch codes, Gunther explaining how he had modified all the surrounding dens to be controlled from the launch console here.

Because Gunther was chatting, I finished entering numbers first. "Now what?" I asked.

Gunther pointed to a squatty, wide console. "All the switches that say, 'Arm'; switch to 'Arm'."

I went over to the console indicated and did as instructed, then turned to Gunther.

"Switches armed."

In the time I had flipped the switches Gunther finished entering codes and was walking towards me and the launch console.

"I think we're ready to launch," Gunther said when he reached me. "They'll hit in just over eight hours. Will that give you enough time to get back to your girl?"

No. It was twelve hours to 'Six. And I was an hour away from 'Atlanta.

Scream of the Ancients

I was two hills away from Gunther's when the first

missile launched. Gunther had told me that the silos were about a mile away, but still I felt the dissonance of the flames with my entire body. It was like a long, drawn out thunder that rolled across the ground instead of the sky. I stopped the cycle and twisted at the torso to see the white trail of smoke pointing to the missile climbing through the blue. It was almost pretty, except I couldn't stop thinking about how those things had radiated the planet for a millennium. I just hoped they worked.

I put another coca leaf in my mouth and started down the dirt path. Another rumble struck me from behind - missile number two, fifteen to go. I kept riding, calculating about how long before they hit the asteroid, then, how long it was going to take me to get to Alina.

I brought the cycle to a stop and put another coca leaf in my mouth, still chewing the previous leaf, as the third missile blew out of its confines. Then I twisted the throttle, kicking up dirt and dust.

Could I be with Alina when the missiles hit? Could I cut off five hours of driving time? There was no way, even if no one was in the tunnels.

I raised up off the seat, using my knees as shock absorbers, and increased speed on the bumpy, dirt path, my thoughts on driving, and Alina. If the missiles did nothing, I could still be with her before the asteroid hit.

The vibrations from missile number four startled me. I had been concentrating on riding and completely forgot about the missiles and the asteroid heading our way. The cycle wiggled between my legs, an unfamiliar wiggle that sent a dagger of terror through me - I thought I was going down. Paint the dirt. Then the path smoothed out and I regained control.

Then number five went up, quickly followed by six, seven and eight. I had to see. I let off the throttle and applied brake. When the cycle slowed I locked the rear tire and skidded a half circle. I switched the engine off and looked to the sky. The rest were all launching. The scene was filled with fire and smoke.

The afternoon sun was bright and warm, the sky cloudless except for the white streaks, each a different length, each pushing a fading missile, each slashing across the otherwise empty sky. I watched for what must have been only minutes but it felt hours. The rumbling in my ears faded slower than the missiles. Then, when I couldn't see flame from any of the missiles, my stomach decided to empty itself. I had chewed too many leaves and nothing else.

I dropped off the cycle and dove for the ground, landing on the grass knees first. I was vomiting before my hands touched. Out came leaf mulch and stomach fluids.

I wiped my lips with my sleeve, angry at myself for getting sick. When was the last time I ate? For that matter, when was the last time I slept? Forty hours? Forty-eight? More? No wonder I was sick.

But I had to get that information to Gunther. I had to push myself to save the planet so I could be with Alina. I blinked: Did I do all this just for me? Didn't I do it for the planet, for everyone living on it? Am I not noble? Am I not the hero? The savior? No, I did it so I could watch the sunsets as Alina and I grow old.

I started to rise, thinking I was finished. My body, though, knew different. Suddenly I pitched forward, hands and knees on the ground again, my gut wrenching, forcing out stale air and a sickening gag over and over. I thought I was going to die of suffocation. I had to breathe!

Concentrating, sweat dripping off my forehead, I stole a breath from my heaving abdomen. The air was hot, burning, tasting of bile. I choked, then heaved even harder, coughing and gagging until I nearly passed out. Seconds lasted hours as I tried vainly to stop the retching, winking in and out of consciousness with each gag.

Then it was over, leaving me on hands and knees gulping lung full after lung full of vomit reeking air, too weak to get up. My head was spinning, nothing was in focus and everything was fading. Moments later I was unconscious. I had pushed too far.

*   *   *

When I awoke I didn't feel rested and refreshed, I felt as tired as I was when I passed out. I still had a sick stomach, now accompanied by a nasty, foul taste in my mouth and a tight head.

I sat up and reached to my head and found that my goggles were still on. I pulled them off and the tightness eased. I looked to the west. It was evening, the sun would be down soon. I had been out about four hours.

Slowly, cautiously, I got to my feet. My head twirled, the horizon dipping first one way, then the next. Thinking I was going to pass out again, I closed my eyes and waited. Waited until things inside my head, and stomach, settled.

Minutes later I opened my eyes, things feeling pretty close to normal. I looked for the missile trails. Flat, thin clouds approached from the west, the sun's angle greying their underside. The missiles were no where in sight. On their way to

Pipe Dreams

the rock from space. I hoped.

    I picked up my goggles then righted the cycle with a bit of effort. My head wouldn't allow me to lean over again to check the cycle for damage, so I glanced before climbing on. The bike looked okay.

    I started the engine. I listened several seconds for trouble as the engine warmed. It sounded fine. I gave it a bit of throttle and listened again. Still fine. I put the goggles on and the cycle in gear and, just before releasing the clutch, put a coca leaf in my mouth. It's bitterness overpowered the flavor of stale bile. My stomach calmed and I began to feel energized. I engaged the clutch.

    As I drove I calculated the time of impact: I will be between 'Two and 'Three when the missiles hit the asteroid, still six, seven hours away from Alina.

    If Alina was right and the missiles have no effect, I won't be in her arms when the end comes. Not now. Even at top speed through the tunnel I couldn't make 'Six in time. If the missiles don't work, these final hours will have been wasted, hours that could have been spent with Alina. My only consolation was that, in the pipe, I won't see the rock coming.

    I have never spent much time pondering love, even after meeting Alina. I haven't thought about what happens to love after years had passed, after we had passed. I've never thought about death that way, only that if you painted the walls of the pipe you couldn't ride anymore.

    But now, as death looms overhead, I realize that other than riding, Alina is my raison d'être. I know there won't be cycles in the next world, but Alina will be there. This I'm certain of.

Pipe Dreams

The Ancient City of Atlanta started to rise out of the horizon and my thoughts shifted to the quickest route through the city to the tunnel. I then wondered about pedestrians in the pipe.

'Atlanta

Riding through the empty streets of the Ancient City of Atlanta during sunset gave me a sense of suspense. I drove on a shadowed street, the low sun filling the intersections with amber light. Another kilometer or so to CCE and the tunnels, I get an unexplained dread that someone or thing was going to dart out in front of me at a cross street. I know the fear was irrational. I know everyone is gone. I maintained my speed, wanting to reach Alina before all hell brook loose, knowing that the missiles will hit when I'm halfway down the pipe.

My stomach tightened as I came to the next intersection. I looked for a shadow from the street on the right and saw none, then turned my attention to the street on the left as I passed. There, standing in the middle, was the small boy from the tunnel. For a horrifying instant, an insane moment of sheer madness, I thought I was going to hit the boy off to my left head on.

I hit both brakes hard, locking up the rear wheel. It lost its grip on the pavement and I was suddenly sliding sideways, steering into the skid. With eyes wide open and probably bulging, I stared at the empty side street now passing in front of me, stunned by what my own mind just did.

By instinct I released the rear brake and the cycle

snapped straight with a wiggle. I stopped half way from the next intersection and shut the engine off, noticing then that I was trembling. Trembling, almost to the point of shivering.

I removed my goggles and rubbed my eyes with my palms, disbelieving the clarity of the hallucination. The boy even had a shadow! I rubbed my eyes harder, trying to clear my mind of the insane thoughts of how the little boy got there.

Then I heard a noise, like footsteps. I dropped my hands from my face to the handlebars, thumb on the starter button, ready to hit it and go. But my vision was momentarily blurry. In that moment a figure walked in front of me and stopped. Thinking it another hallucination I simply waited until the blurriness went away, and the hallucination with it.

As my sight cleared, however, a small, tired old man came into focus. He was shorter than I was sitting on the cycle, but he was bent over at the waist, a crooked back forcing him that way. His skin was ladened with wrinkles, a sun hardened hide. I jumped when he spoke to me.

"What the shit are you doing here, boy?" His voice was as coarse as he looked.

I stared at the old man, dumbfounded. I didn't know hallucinations could talk.

"I said, Boy, what the shit are you doing here?" he repeated with more growl.

He is real. What is *he* doing here? And where did he come from? "I'm Ben. A Rider for C.."

"I can sees you're a Rider, boy. That don't answer my shit question. What are you doing here? Everyone else took off 'cause of that shit rock going to hit."

"I just..." Wait, wait. What was I explaining to him for?

Pipe Dreams

"No. Who are you, and what are you doing here?" I demanded.

"I ain't got to tell you shit, boy. And if you ain't gonna talk to me, get the shit out of my way."

We stared at each other for a moment. Daring the other to do something.

I looked him over. The white hair on his head was dirty and knotted, clumps jutting out like little trees. His eyes were brown and staring through me; they were filled with anger. His hands were twisted and distorted, fingers pointing the wrong way with swollen knuckles. They hung off thin and fragile arms, held close to his thin body so as not to catch the breeze.

He looked defeated, as if a good wind could blow him over and put him out of his misery. Then he moved towards me, a bad knee causing a waddle in his walk. I sat there amazed he didn't break by the effort.

"I'm waiting for the shit rock to hit, boy," he said as he went by.

I could smell his breath, it stank of rotted teeth. I turned and looked over my shoulder at him, but he was gone. I blinked hard, trying to bring him back. But the street remained empty. This was going to make the ride back very interesting.

I hit the start button and fired up the engine. I released the clutch, the front tire leaving the ground as I sped away. I concentrate on riding, pushing all other thoughts out of my mind. Even Alina.

CCE was just ahead. I thought about sleeping there, having decided that it was the lack of sleep and food causing these hallucinations. I dismissed the coca leaves because I still wanted to ride for twelve more hours and needed their boost. I did not want to sleep, though. If the missiles did work as planned, I could be with Alina by time the skip occurred. If the asteroid was going to hit I wanted to be on my cycle, in the pipe, dreaming. But I could eat.

When I reached CCE I parked the cycle and went to the kitchen. The pillaging went quick: When they had evacuated they had taken all the supplies. I found only a dry roll and a palm-sized piece of rabbit jerky in the pantry. Off a shelf I selected a goblet and filled it with water before returning to my cycle, eating the morsels on the way.

I sat the goblet on the floor between the tunnels, put a leaf between my teeth, then shot down the westbound pipe. Twelve hours to 'Six and security in the grasp of Alina's arms. I sucked the leaf to the back of my mouth and began to chew it, the bitterness kicking me out of a drowsiness I didn't realize I was falling into. Twelve more hours.

RS-1

The run to RS-1 is fairly straight, yet I dare not nap, knowing with certainty that I would not awaken if the cycle twitched. But I could open the throttle.

The amber lights inside the pipe quickly blur as I accelerate. I fall into a zone, driving by habit, riding by instinct. The power of the coca leaf circulates through me and I feel *on*, all-powerful. I push the tachometer into the red, all thoughts of mortality absent.

This is what I live for, to ride. The wind in my face, the maneuvers at the bends, the sensation of control, and the thrill of speed. It is now, when I'm in the Zone, does life feel right.

Pipe Dreams

Now, when I concentrate on driving, do I feel at peace. Now, when the solitude in the tunnel wraps me in myself, do I feel at one with the world. It is also now that hours turn into minutes, seconds into days as my mind, consciously occupied with the task of riding the cycle, drifts into worlds of fantasy, memories, and pipe dreams.

It is also now, too, that I miss Alina. I dream of her, want her. I fantasize about being with her, living with her at the observatory. She is what fills me with happiness and, no matter how much I like my solitude, she has caused me to love, to yearn for the presence of another.

I swallow the remnants of the coca leaf, missing Alina as I've never missed her before, wishing this was already over and I was watching her watch the stars at her telescope.

While arguing with myself whether or not I should pop in another leaf, the platform for 'One came into view. I wouldn't stop until I reached Alina if it wasn't for need of fuel. I pulled onto the platform moments later and quickly refueled the cycle, getting back in the tunnel within minutes. I know I was pushing the cycle just as much as myself, either of us possible of breaking down any moment, but I had to get back to Alina. Had to! I pushed extraneous thoughts out of my head and put another leaf in my mouth, twisting the throttle full open.

The run from 'One to 'Two is the most demanding of the pipe and I wanted to get it over with, wishing I was between 'Five and 'Six. As I came to the first of many curves and bends I remembered the little boy I almost hit just hours ago. The memory sent a chill through me, then I was at the curve and I fell into my zone: All thoughts are shut out, nothing is recognized except the pipe and getting through it one more time.

RS-2

At RS-2 I stepped outside and relieved myself. It was evening, dark, the black sky filled with stars. I zipped up my windsuit then looked for, and located, the asteroid. I strained to find the missiles, unsure if I saw seventeen glowing points near it or not. I stared at the luminous falling body, its tail longer and pointing the rock right to us.

Back inside and on the cycle I started a new leaf, even though a voice told me not to chew any more leaves. A soft, little voice, that also urged me to ride outside.

I dismissed both suggestions, the need to get to Alina an obsession. The front wheel left the pipe as I started off, the back tire chirping with each change of gear.

This run winds down, or up the mountain range, depending on which direction you are going. I was going down, the fast direction. Usually I love riding through this part of the pipe, and between 'One and 'Two for that matter, but I'm tired, exhausted.

The run from 'One to 'Two had taken a lot out of me. If it wasn't for the leaves from the Hermit I would be asleep somewhere, perhaps even painted on the tunnel walls. I ground the leaf between my back teeth as I dug for another one, wanting to be sure I was awake and not going to do any painting.

The first curve is coming up, an S-curve followed by a sharp downhill bend. I start my swing up the wall, going left first, almost to the amber lights. My timing is impeccable, the guide marks having not been cleaned off this far east helped. Up and around I went, but as I crossed the top I had a horrible feeling something was wrong.

I had hit the first curve too fast, slamming the suspension hard as I came out of it into the downhill bend. I bounced off the top, myself shaken from the blow. But I must have hit it at angle because it was all I could do to right the cycle on the way to the bottom. The cycle did hit the bottom tires first, but it hit hard. Hard enough to cause me to blackout for a moment. I can't rightly say how I held on nor how I stayed up, but I did.

I settled on the bottom of the pipe, headed downhill faster than the cycle is suppose to go, blaming the second leaf for my lapse in judgment when a pain began heating up in the middle of my lower back.

I had, apparently, slammed myself as well as the cycle. I tried to move, bend at the waist but was stopped when a hot blade stuck me in the middle of my back. I knew then I had done damage. I knew I had just received one of those debilitating Rider's injuries. The old man in 'Atlanta zipped through my thoughts on a cycle.

Although it was painful to try to bend, my back seemed just fine driving the cycle. Only a warm spot that throbbed. I didn't allow myself to think what would happen about the next stop when I had to dismount. I did, however, slow a bit after the tunnel leveled off.

RS-3

Pipe Dreams

When the platform for 'Three was in sight I started thinking about how I was going to refuel. I gently, gingerly, moved at the waist. The hot blade I felt earlier returned instantly. This was not going to be easy.

I pulled onto the platform and stopped next to the fueling line. I shut the engine off, then reached for the nozzle with my right arm. The hot blade not only stabbed me again, but it was bigger and went deeper. I snapped my arm back and yelped in agony, the cry echoing down the tunnel. I held myself upright with my left arm, hand on the tank, as tears ran down my cheeks, the pain excruciating. My right arm hung limp at my side, numb. I silently cursed myself for messing up. How could I ride now? How am I going to get to Alina? Is..is she still going to want me, now?

Then, out of some twisted logic, I slowly leaned to the left, bending at the waist, until something snapped. It was a loud, dull crack that sent the hot blade up my spine to my neck and right shoulder. Again I screamed in pain, tears again flowing in rivulets. But the numbness in my right arm was gone, replaced with a discomfort that made me wish it was numb again. Then the door to the outside opened.

I couldn't turn around to see who it was, so I started pushing the cycle backwards to the door when I heard a small voice say, "Wha' 'cha doin', Mister?"

The little body belonging to the small voice walked around in front of me. I wondered if he was the little boy in tunnel I almost hit before. He looked to be around ten years old and he had transparent eyes.

"I heard ya' hollerin' and came to see who was dyin'."

"Not dying. Just wishing so."

The boy smiled.

"Think you could hand me the fuel nozzle?"

He looked at the refueling station, then at me. "Sure."

During the refueling the boy told me that he had seen a flash where the asteroid was just a short time ago. It had to have been the missiles. I couldn't get how long ago it had happened, but I did know that if the missiles did not work to deflect the asteroid we would be finding out soon.

I pressed on, still wanting to be in the pipe if the rock did hit. I never once thought about who was taking care of the boy as the amber lights became one.

RS-4; 5

The run to 'Four is unbent and boring. Again, to keep from falling asleep I lock the throttle and fly down the pipe, gnawing on a leaf. The spot on my back warms, enlarging, spreading all the way across and halfway to my shoulder blades. It sort of feels good, like a hot, wet towel placed across my back. I leave my arms off the handlebars. I'm flying.

Halfway to RS-4 I realize that the missiles must have deflected the asteroid and that we were safe, else it would have hit by now. I grabbed the hand grips and slowed down a little, down to cruising speed. I had a bit more time now.

Minutes after easing up I thought I saw a silhouette ahead. There couldn't be. Not again. Not now. Why didn't the boy warn me?

Instinctively I start to pendulum, not even considering slowing down, not even sure I saw someone. During the third time across the bottom I saw the figure ahead. It looked like a woman, a grown woman half as tall as the pipe. She was standing still, facing me, her eyes wide and mouth agape. This was going to be a little different than with the boy, the woman was taller.

As I approached the terrified woman I saw how to make it past her: Instead of going over the top of her, which would cause us to knock heads, I thought that I would fit if I rode the lights, at either ninety or one-eighty. I adjusted speed and my swing, passing her moments later. As I passed I could hear her screaming.

I couldn't look back to see how she was doing and it was a good thing I couldn't because there was another person in the tunnel. He was just as scared as the woman I just passed, but his scream was louder. I passed him the same way but on the other side.

Sweat was soaking my underclothes as I came upon yet another fool in the pipe. She too, was scared stiff, but silent as I passed on her left.

When I didn't come across anyone else for several seconds I thought those three were it. Then I saw him - running. Oh, the idiot. He had no idea how difficult he was going to make this. The timing was going to be a little more tricky, especially if he decides to stop or, my heart stuttered when the thought came: What if he tries to dart out of the way? Which way would he go?

Seconds before reaching the running fool, I had to choose on which side of him to pass. The seconds went much too fast and I went left. Habit.

As I passed him, my head and the cycle even with his

head, out of the corner of my eye I saw him grab for me. I then felt a jerk and the rear of the cycle fell to the bottom of the pipe, hitting with a jolt. Instantly I released throttle and turned toward the bottom, fishtailing as I fought going unconscious from the burning pain in my back brought on by the jolt.

    Ninety agonizing seconds later I had control of the cycle and the pain in my back, the latter with help from two more leafs. I didn't dare look back to see how the fool was, there might still be more. Then, as RS-4 loomed in the distance I began to wonder if there would be any one there to assist me with the fuel.

    During the last minutes to 'Four I tormented myself for having messed up my back and possibly the rest of my life with Alina, the fact that the missiles had to have worked never entering my mind.

    One of the two fueling hoses at RS-4 was out of its holster and hanging down within easy reach of my crippled ass. Still, there was pain as I handled the hose. I added a fresh leaf to the two nearly pulverized in my mouth to help ease the extra pain. Four more hours and a bit more luck at 'Five for fueling and I'll be in the arms of my Alina, escaping the pain in sleep.

    With the tank topped off I adjusted my goggles over my eyes, put my right foot on the foot peg, and pulled in the clutch lever. Just as I touched my finger to the starter button the tunnel and platform shuttered as if the ground were shaking, but it only happened the one time. A quick jolt that was sent up the pipe from ahead like something big had struck the tunnel. I thought perhaps another Rider painted the walls, but the jolt was too strong for that to be the cause. It was past time for the asteroid.

Pipe Dreams

I pushed the starter button and the engine growled into life as another jolt shook the tunnel. My mind raced through possibilities while I maneuvered back into the pipe. I felt another shot to the pipe as I passed over the threshold of the platform. Could some of the missiles have fallen back to Earth? No, they would have been in pieces. I twisted the throttle and continued on with the next leg of my insane journey, bewildered by the jolts to the tunnel, a foreboding growing as I gained speed. I felt three more shocks to the pipe before reaching final gear, then none thereafter.

At 'Five there were two people, a man and a woman enwrapped in each other, as I pulled onto the platform. That they didn't hear the cycle is testimony to their enrapture. My headlights, however, startled them like deer on a path at night. I was giggling uncontrollably when I shut off the engine, somehow managing a "Sorry" between snickers.

"What are you doing riding?" the male of the couple asked. They were in their early twenties, she an inch or two shorter than he, both with clear hair.

"Just trying to get home." I looked him in the eye, he didn't feel threatened. Good. "Could you help me fuel up the cycle?" I patted the tank of my cycle, somehow feeling closer to the machine now. "I sprained my back and it's a little difficult to get off and on this thing."

While the couple was whispering away and studying me over, I raised my goggles and wiped my hands over my face. I felt spent, exhausted, nothing left. But RS-6 was the next stop. Two more hours. Another leaf. Two?

I heard movement, then the man said, "Sure."

I dropped my hands from my face, he was walking

towards me.

"Show me what to do?" he said when he was between me and the fueling station.

As my tank was filling I asked them if they had felt the jolts. I almost didn't ask, figuring if they didn't hear the cycle, why should they feel those. But they had.

"We were outside on our way here," the woman said, "when we saw falling stars. There was a bunch of them."

"A shower," the man interrupted. The tank on the cycle was full and he was replacing the nozzle. "It looked like some of them hit."

Something caught in my throat and I coughed, a singe of pain shooting around my waist. I winced. Was that what shook the pipe? He was wrong. They didn't hit. Couldn't have hit. I had to get to 'Six.

"You okay?" she asked.

She must have noticed my change in color. "Yeah." I sucked in air as I reached up and lowered my goggles. "I just need to get home."

I thanked them both and started the cycle, then moved into the pipe and made the rear tire scream. The foreboding from earlier now an unknown terror. At the first straight-away I started two more leaves.

RS-6

An hour from 'Six, just before I reached the S-curve, I noticed fresh air, outside air; something was wrong. No. It's the access panel I left open less than a day ago. But there was also an unfamiliar scent to the air. The aroma crisp, metallic, like something had burned. Suddenly the smell increased, as if I had gone through a wall of the stench. I coughed, expelling the leaf mulch, only to catch up with it a moment later.

As I entered the S-curve the air freshened. I was close to an opening. Panic attempted a coup dè tat using the foreign chemicals coursing through me as I headed up the left wall as the pipe turned to the right. Where was the opening? How big was it? What caused it? I crossed the top and had every question answered.

There ahead of me as the pipe curved back to the left, was the entrance and exit openings of what had to be a meteorite strike. They cut across the pipe at a sixty-degree angle. Debris covered the bottom at the openings.

The entry hole was a jagged mouth of steel fangs and concrete teeth. I downshifted then twisted the throttle, shooting over the top of the exit hole on the lower right as I kissed the gauges to make sure I missed the lowest tooth from the entry opening above me.

Surprisingly, I wasn't shaken up by that relatively minor obstruction. It did occur to me, however, that the missiles must have broke off some pieces of asteroid and that is what hit the pipe.

Wondering if there was anymore damage, I rode on towards the eight kilometer downhill slide. I had felt more than one jolt back at 'Four. There had to be more damage, more holes ahead. I should have slowed down. But I didn't. The other holes *had* to be in the other tunnel.

I came to the downhill bend and rolled up to the top as the pipe turned down, coming out as usual to a pendulum swing on the bottom. Only as I went up the left side on one of my pendulum swings, my left handgrip nicked a dent in the pipe. The cycle wobbled a frightening dance. I was sure I was going down, at close to maximum speed, too. I was going to paint the walls!

Then, with a grimace and a scream to the wind for the pain in my back, I gained control of the cycle and smoothly went up the other side. Breathing again as I headed down, my back on fire.

Illuminated by my headlights was a staggered row of jagged concrete stalactites dangling to my left. The concrete was cracked and hung down almost a meter, suspended by the metal rod reinforcement. Air filtered through the larger cracks. Dust and debris littered the deck.

I put more rubber on the pipe as I slowed to steer through the debris. I close to the gauges to stay clear of the concrete teeth. Suddenly I was nervous, frightened of the pipe for the first time.

Thirty seconds later the dents stopped, but dust and debris had rolled all the way to the bottom of the hill. So what usually takes a minute and a half took me over five, finally clearing the debris field several hundred meters after leveling out.

This should have been a clear indicator for me to slow down, but being so close to home, so full of coca leaf, so exhausted, that I looked on the positive side. I completely forgot the foreboding earlier, and decided that that was all there was for damage.

When I didn't see anymore dust I twisted the throttle 'til the cable was taut. It was straight for an hour, but I was going to see how much under that hour I could be. Again I leaned to the gauges, to cut wind resistance. Again, the warmth in my back grew hotter and bigger, but I was almost in Alina's arms. I did my best to ignore the pain with another leaf.

Then a silly thought came to me, undoubtedly brought on by the lack of sleep. I thought that, maybe if Alina walked on my back she could pop back in whatever popped out. I smiled, the wind catching my cheek and making it flap.

I rode; awake too long, too many leafs consumed, and way too much speed. I dropped into the zone. My thoughts ticked by as quickly as the amber lights on either side of me; from Alina to my parents to Seth to the little boy standing in the tunnel to the running fool and back to Alina. Seems lately my thoughts always return to her. But that is as it should be, your mind always resting on memories of the one you love.

I rode, Alina filtering through my zone until she was behind me, her arms tightly around my waist, holding me close with her head against me. The burning pain in my lower back was gone, her touch somehow making it stop. Too, my exhaustion had vanished. Again, because of her touch.

Vanished, too, was the top of the tunnel, exposing the stars. The air smelled wonderful; fresh, clean, and of the desert. I filled my lungs with the gritty ether, expanding my chest to its fullest. Alina let go, disappearing instead of falling off. Then I tasted metal in the air.

I blinked. A heartbeat away was a gap in the pipe. I had no idea if I could jump the gap and panicked, closing my eyes and pulling back on the handlebars just as the front tire reached the edge.

The cycle lifted into the midnight air and silence

surrounded me. I couldn't hear the engine nor the wind. My mind went blank with the calm. Time distorted, a single hour stretching the length of the gap. It was taking too long.

My mind clicked on, horrible thoughts of not making it to the other side racing through. Incredibly, I wished for a quick death.

Then I was on the other side, headless, my body and cycle riding on down the tunnel towards RS-6 and Alina, my head rolling off the outside of the pipe.

I landed hard on the other side, the bottom of the frame scratched the deck with a slamming jolt. I came down on the fuel tank as the cycle was coming back up from the first bounce. Instantly came this tremendous agony from my groin, simultaneously that hot blade in my back cut up the length of my spine, body wide.

I remember hearing this loud, awful, sad noise while I watched instinct release the throttle and apply both brakes. Locking my elbows against the forward momentum, I realized that the noise was myself attempting a breathless scream. My eyes involuntarily closed, I was going to paint the walls.

A Mural

Into my darkness came a familiar voice, a male voice. "It looks like he's finally waking up."

Finally? How long was I asleep? Who was he talking to? Alina? I felt terrible. My head hurt as if it had been beaten on with a hammer. My back, no longer on fire, was now numb, almost like I was laying on air. My right arm ached and hung above my chest in a sling, my left I couldn't feel, nor could I feel any sensation in my legs. I opened my eyes, slamming them shut when the light entered.

"You awake, Benjamin?" A voice asked.

I knew that voice. It didn't bring any comfort, though.

"He's awake," the voice confirmed to someone in the room. "Go get Doc."

Quentin. That's who it was. I opened my eyes again. Slowly, letting the light bleed in a little at a time. Then I heard footfalls leave the room, then the Quentin asked me, "Where did the finger come from?"

"Wa-.." I forced saliva, then swallowed best I could. "Water," I whispered dryly. Who did he ask to go get Doc? Seth?

Quentin helped me sit up enough to drink from a wooden goblet, the cool water dancing down my throat.

"Thanks," I said after Quentin laid me back down. "What finger?" I asked quietly, the effort to talk taxing. I tried to remember what had happened.

"The one we found on the back of your cycle. It was stuck in the frame," Quentin explained.

I listened to Quentin walk away as the running fool in the tunnel flashed into my mind. That moment he grabbed for me and the cycle jerked. It had to be his finger. Then I heard drapes being pulled and the light dimmed.

"You should be able to find," I paused for several breaths, the sound of Quentin's footsteps booming in the humming silence, "the owner of the finger at either 'Three or 'Four." Again I had to catch up with my breathing. "I don't remember which I was closer to at the time."

"That happened in the tunnel?" Quentin sounded astounded.

The tunnel! That's right. I had been in the pipe, riding to 'Six when the tunnel...the tunnel..a round mouth with jagged teeth of concrete and metal rods was rapidly approaching me...the tunnel..tried to eat me. The asteroid! The meteor damage to the pipe. Then I had a most horrible thought; How much damage did the meteors do?

"Where's Alina?" I looked to the door. "Where's Seth?" I asked. I heard Quentin suck in air. His back was to the window so I couldn't see his face, but I got the distinct impression that he didn't want to answer my question.

"The Star Gazers out here were watching the asteroid when they saw the missiles explode. Pieces of the asteroid broke off when the missiles hit it." This was going to be bad news. "The asteroid changed direction enough to deflect off our atmosphere at a point that caused a meteor shower to rain on the Ice north of RS-3.

"The pieces that broke off came down and hit the tunnels between RS-5 and RS-7. RS-5 was undamaged."

I didn't like the way he paused.

"RS-6 was hit," he paused again. After a moment of utter silence to let the meaning sink in, Quentin added, "Pieces also hit RS-7. But, that was all the damage. Your gamble worked, Benjamin. Almost."

I closed my eyes in a vain attempt to stop the flow of tears. Quietly, so I wouldn't burst out bawling, I asked, "What about 'Six? What happened to Alina? Seth?"

Quentin forced a cough. "Seth is at RS-6, now. He's heading the rebuilding project for his Stop. They've already started clearing away debris..."

"Where's Alina?" I had tried to shout it at him, scream it at him, but it embarrassingly squeaked out.

Silence. A horrible, dreadful silence. Then Quentin spoke quietly, solemnly to the floor. "She's dead. The observatory and surrounding area was hit with several pieces." He turned quickly and walked to the door, not looking at me once.

If I could have moved either arm I would have pulled out every tube stuck in me and let my life drain onto the floor. I didn't want to go on without Alina. Again, the old man in 'Atlanta raced through my mind on a flaming cycle.

Then the door opened. Doc and a young woman with auburn hair entered the room and came directly to my bed.

*   *   *

Eighteen months have passed since Gunther and I, without authorization, launched the missiles to deflect the asteroid. It has been three months since I was let out of that damn bed and that ugly city. I have seen Gunther twice in those three months. Both times we convinced each other we did the right thing. Everyone is still alive. Most everyone.

The missiles did indeed deflect the asteroid, and the asteroid did skip off the atmosphere like a flat stone on a still pond, saving us from total destruction. But there were those pieces that chipped off. They were the ones that killed Alina, and many others.

The spill I took at the gap worsened the four compressed vertebrae I received at that S-curve near RS-2. It caused paralysis in my legs for a year.

Pipe Dreams

My right shoulder had been torn from the socket and the arm broke below the elbow. I still can't raise it over my head. My left arm healed with little complications.

A concussion put me into a coma that lasted two weeks. I had other bruises and cuts, but nothing to write about.

Seth came to visit, twice, when he wasn't too busy with the rebuilding project. He has since been put in charge of rebuilding everything, from 'Six to 'Seven. I've also seen him twice since leaving 'Tucson. We don't talk a whole lot when we see each other. He talks about the rebuilding project. I usually comment on the weather.

I live in the ruins of the observatory at 'Six. I won't let Seth rebuild it. I know it probably sounds strange, but I feel closer to Alina there as it is. She still awaits my return. That's why I ride, now and again. I'm still trying to get back to her, into her arms, those eyes.

Twice in the past two months I've gone to see the Hermit, then gotten hold of a cycle. I ride the pipes. Thirty-six hours the first time, forty-three the second.

When I ride I think about when I was riding to save the world. Save it for me and Alina. But, she's gone now. Too, are my dreams. The only thing left is to ride, now and again.

But my mind seems to wander a lot more now. To unanswerable questions. Like why the asteroid turned west and not east? Why our ancestors, with their technical prowess, didn't come up with something to stop incoming rocks instead of nearly destroying the one we live on? Why did the asteroid come at all? Are there beings out there in the blackness of space knocking them our way? Will they send another?

I also think about missing that little boy on the way to

Pipe Dreams

Gunther's, and missing the others on the way back.

Why didn't I become a mural and paint the walls eighteen months ago? Was the old man in 'Atlanta me to be? And I think about where Alina is, wondering where she waits. And, I wonder what lies beyond our realm?

But I must go. I went to the Hermit yesterday. More coca leaves and that aromatic smoke. CCE thinks I make these runs for nostalgia.

I put two leaves in my mouth and bite down as I release the clutch, the rear tire leaving a black streak in the pipe entrance. The amber lights blur as I push the cycle to maximum speed. Then my mind torments me.

Quentin had said that the observatories were watching the approach of the rock and saw the missiles impact. That meant that Alina had been watching, too.

I wonder if she saw the pieces coming towards her, figuring trajectory on a notepad on her knee? I shudder, then swallow the leaf mulch as I dig for another.